· LOOK AND FIND ·

Disney's
Beauty
and the
Beast

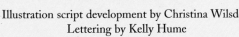
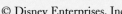
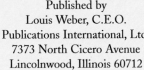

**Look and Find art illustrated
by Jaime Diaz Studios**

Illustration script development by Christina Wilsdon
Lettering by Kelly Hume

© Disney Enterprises, Inc.

Published by
Louis Weber, C.E.O.
Publications International, Ltd.
7373 North Cicero Avenue
Lincolnwood, Illinois 60712

www.pubint.com

Look and Find is a trademark of
Publications International, Ltd.

Manufactured in China.

8 7 6 5 4 3 2 1

ISBN 0-7853-4151-X

Once upon a time, there was a kind and beautiful girl named Belle who taught an enchanted Beast how to love and earn the love of others.

Take a look at the world of Beauty and the Beast. It is full of adventure and romance. Can you find these characters from this wonderful story?

Belle

The Beast

Gaston

Maurice

Lumiere

Cogsworth

Mrs. Potts

It's a hustle-bustle morning in the village and Belle is off to visit the bookstore—again. She's an odd girl who loves to read, but Gaston doesn't mind. He plans to marry her whether she wants him or not!

Can you find Belle and Gaston? Can you find these other people in the village, too?

Belle

Le Fou

Gaston

The butcher

The chimney sweep

The baker

The triplets

The bookseller

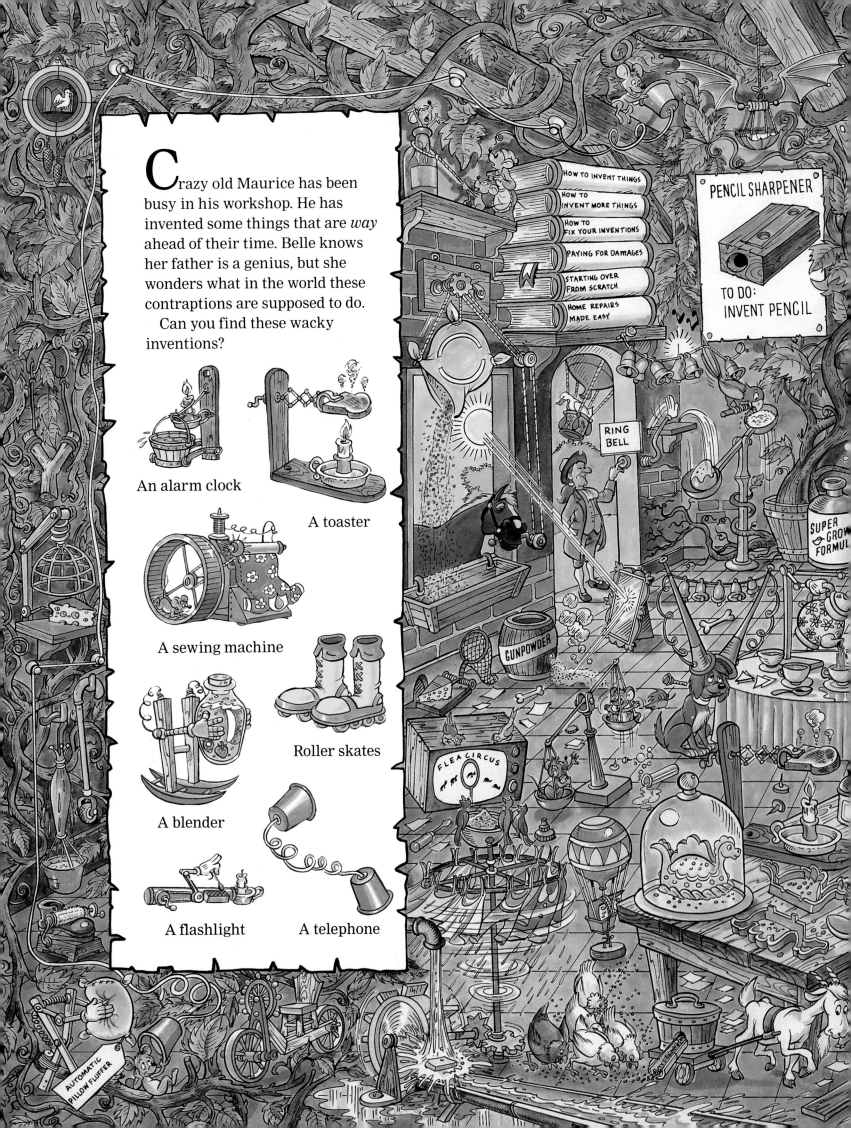

Crazy old Maurice has been busy in his workshop. He has invented some things that are *way* ahead of their time. Belle knows her father is a genius, but she wonders what in the world these contraptions are supposed to do.

Can you find these wacky inventions?

An alarm clock

A toaster

A sewing machine

Roller skates

A blender

A flashlight

A telephone

PENCIL SHARPENER

TO DO: INVENT PENCIL

HOW TO INVENT THINGS
HOW TO INVENT MORE THINGS
HOW TO FIX YOUR INVENTIONS
PAYING FOR DAMAGES
STARTING OVER FROM SCRATCH
HOME REPAIRS MADE EASY

RING BELL

SUPER GROW FORMUL[A]

GUNPOWDER

FLEA CIRCUS

AUTOMATIC PILLOW FLUFFER

Gaston hoped his marriage proposal would make a splash, but this isn't exactly what he had in mind! As for Belle, she thinks Gaston is all washed up.

Take a look around Belle's little farm. Can you find these ladies who *do* have eyes for Gaston?

Mademoiselle Mule

Giselle Goose

Portia Pig

Eunice Ewe

Henrietta Hen

Colette Cow

HUMPTY DUMPTY WAS PUSHED!

The Beast has everything his heart desires...almost. If only he had someone to love who would love him back and break the spell. Until the day she arrives, the Beast's only companions are his enchanted servants.

Can you find these members of the Beast's household?

Lumiere

Cogsworth

Coatrack

Mrs. Potts

Chip

Footstool

Featherduster

HOW TO MAKE FRIENDS

MEET GIRLS

Gaston thinks he's a fine specimen of a man—and when he brags, people listen! Don't plug *your* ears, either, if you know what's good for you.

Any minute now, Gaston will notice that he's missing a few things. Can you find them?

His foolish friend

His mirror

A letter from his mother

His quiver

His blunderbuss

His comb

A picture of his favorite person

Belle doesn't have much of an appetite tonight, but Mrs. Potts and Lumiere are sure they can tempt her to try just a tiny bite of something. Perhaps a little music will help.

Can you find these tempting morsels that the kitchen has whipped up for Belle's first supper in the castle?

Caesar salad

Aged cheese

Angel food cake

French bread

Chilled asparagus

Chicken à la king

Atten-*shun!* Gaston's angry mob is sure the Beast is a terrible monster. Now everyone in the castle, from the lowliest dustbin to the fanciest featherduster, must report for duty to protect the Beast and his castle.

Look for these soldiers as they battle the villagers.

General Junque

Private Pillowfight

Lieutenant Ladle

Brigadier Buckethead

Sergeant Snipp

Corporal Cookpot

Admiral Armor

The Beast was not the only enchanted person living in the magical castle. When Belle helped turn him back into a Prince, the enchanted objects turned back into their real selves, too.

Can you find these members of the Beast's household who are feeling like themselves again?

Cogsworth

Lumiere

Footstool

Chip

Mrs. Potts

Featherduster

Wardrobe

Go back to Belle's village to find these characters who have their noses in books.

- ☐ A cat reading *Puss in Boots*
- ☐ A girl reading *Cinderella*
- ☐ A cook reading a cookbook
- ☐ A nursemaid reading *Mother Goose*
- ☐ A boy reading a diary
- ☐ A frog reading *The Frog Prince*

Take a closer look at the world of Belle and the Beast. Can you find these characters, too?

- ☐ Philippe
- ☐ Le Fou
- ☐ Chip
- ☐ The pretty triplets
- ☐ Featherduster
- ☐ Footstool

Go back to the tavern. Can you find these happy-go-lucky fellows?

- ☐ A fellow walking on his hands
- ☐ A fellow with an eye patch
- ☐ A fellow with a fish in his back pocket
- ☐ A fellow wearing five hats
- ☐ A fellow with a rope for a belt
- ☐ A fellow snoozing

Maurice is trying to build a better mousetrap. Go back to his workshop to find these attempts.

- ☐ A cage trap
- ☐ A glass jar trap
- ☐ A butterfly net trap
- ☐ A balloon trap
- ☐ A mixing bowl trap
- ☐ A cat trap

1,000s

OF FACTS, THINGS, PEOPLE, PLACES, AND ANIMALS THAT ARE SIMPLY

DISGUSTING

PaRragon

Bath · New York · Singapore · Hong Kong · Cologne · Delhi · Melbourne

Consultants: Sally Morgan, Dr. Ben Robinson, Philip Parker, and
Ade Scott-Colson
Cartoons created by Rob Davis and Guy Harvey
Models by Sue Hunter-Jones
Photography by Martin Haswell

This edition produced by Tall Tree Ltd, London

First published by Parragon in 2009
Parragon
Queen Street House
4 Queen Street
Bath BA1 1HE, UK

ISBN 978-1-4075-1588-5

Printed in China

1,000s

OF FACTS, THINGS, PEOPLE, PLACES, AND ANIMALS THAT ARE SIMPLY

DISGUSTING

Moira Butterfield

PaRragon

Bath · New York · Singapore · Hong Kong · Cologne · Delhi · Melbourne

Contents

Oh my old man, what have you been eating?

Icky Introduction

Imagine a grimy, stinky place full of slimy creatures…Yes, it's YOUR bedroom! If even your own room is yucky, imagine just how much disgustingness there is in the whole world!

This book contains a bumper collection of foul facts that prove our planet is really just a puss-filled zit on the pimply face of the universe, and we humans are basically walking bags of boogers, flakes, and farty gas. What's not to enjoy?

Sicko sections include shocking secrets of history, the stinky human body (yes, you), and some gross chapters on animals, creepie-crawlies, science, the world, your horrible home, and the terrible truth about what you eat (don't read that one before supper).

To keep you busy, there are also lots of disgusting experiments and things to make.

However, the main purpose of this book isn't to make you throw up. It's to make you laugh. So sit down, choose a chapter, and have fun, farty pants!

History Smells

CRAZY CAVEMEN

Our ancient ancestors were probably hairy, ugly, and smelly—just like our relatives today, in fact! It seems early humans were big on murdering, eating flesh, and painting with spit.

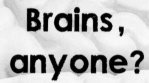

Brains, anyone?

The oldest modern human skulls ever found date to about 160,000 years ago. They turned up in Ethiopia and may hold a grisly secret about what was on the menu back then. The skulls had cut marks on them, which shows that the flesh had been carved off—possibly by cannibals who liked to tuck into their neighbors for dinner.

He died dreaming

Inside Tollund Man (right) experts found his last meal—vegetable porridge and a type of fungus that would have given him hallucinations (weird dreams while awake) before he died.

Early humans liked to create cave paintings—using dirt or charcoal mixed with spit, animal fat, or urine!

Murder mysteries

Some ancient sites have turned out to be more like TV murder crime scenes. **Tollund Man, a 2,000-year-old murder victim**, was discovered in a peat bog in Denmark in 1950. He had been hanged with rope and deliberately dumped in the bog, perhaps as a human sacrifice to a goddess. The bog preserved his body and made him leathery-looking. And a 5,000-year-old victim, Otzi the Iceman, was found preserved in ice in the Alps. He probably died after some kind of gang fight between rival tribes. He had been shot in the back with an arrow, was covered in cuts, and had other people's blood on him.

Icky evolution

Scientists say that our first ancestors were **slimy sea creatures**. Modern humans evolved (developed) from hairy, apelike creatures. The human-apes did better than ordinary apes because they had bigger bums.* That meant they could run faster, so they hunted better. Because they were top hunters they guzzled lots of the brain-boosting protein found in meat and got smarter and smarter.

*It's true. Monkeys don't have big bums. Compare the size of human bum cheeks to a monkey's bum next time you go to the zoo.

REALLY ROTTEN ROMANS

Most of Europe was ruled by the Romans 2,000 years ago. They had some of the most disgusting habits ever to turn up in our history books.

Roman priests predicted the future by studying the freshly pulled-out innards of sacrificed animals.

A disgusting day out

Romans loved nothing better than a day watching violent death at the games. The **Colosseum in Rome** was the most famous sports super-stadium, where gladiators fought to the death. They were mostly slaves who had no choice but to train and fight. Winners got big money prizes, but losers were often killed in front of the cheering crowds. After a killing, a referee came out to hit the corpse over the head with a mallet. This showed that the victim now belonged to the god Pluto, king of the dead.

Pass the sponge

Roman public restrooms were a line of holes in a long stone seat set over running water. People wiped themselves with a sponge on a stick.

Massive menus

Roman nobles were famous for holding huge **banquets** and trying to outdo each other with amazing food, most of which sounds really gross. The meals might take up to eight hours. It was considered polite to belch, and if guests didn't want to leave the table, they could get a slave to bring them a vase to pee in. On the right are some of the strange dishes you might expect on an over-the-top Roman menu.

Menu

Come to dinner at Marcus's house!
Hope you're hungry!

❖ Roast pig stuffed with live birds that will fly out when you cut the pig open

❖ Pig's udder stuffed with oysters

❖ Goatfish (allowed to die slowly at the table because it turns a pretty color as it dies)

❖ Sauce made from rotten fish

❖ Guests to eat lying down

❖ Vases for peeing in will be supplied when required

Welcome to the one and only Col-oss-eum! Your entertainment for today features death, dismemberment, and lots of blood. Have a nice day!

In lunch breaks at the Colosseum, criminals were shoved into a no-win fight with animals, such as lions and tigers.

Project

STABBED BY MY ENEMIES!

One of the main hobbies of important Romans was killing each other to get to the top job of emperor. The most famous emperor, Julius Caesar, was famously stabbed by his so-called friends. Next time you go to a costume party, dress up as Caesar with a convincing knife in his back.

- White craft glue or double-side
- Scissors
- Cardboard—a strip 16 in. x 12 in. for the dagger blade, and two T-shape pieces for the dagger handle.
- Aluminum foil strips
- Ruler
- Paint, colored paper, or colored masking tape
- A soft, narrow fabric belt
- A rectangular cardboard box roughly 6 in. x 4½ in. x 28 in. (such as a crispbread box or similar food box)
- An old white sheet, safety pins, and some red paint for the rest of the outfit

1 Make a fold in one end of the dagger blade, about ³/₄ inch from the bottom. Wrap foil around the dagger above the fold.

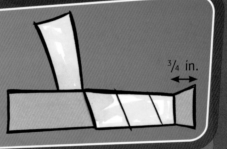

³/₄ in.

2 Tape or glue the dagger handle pieces on either side of the dagger blade and paint or cover with colored paper.

3 Open up one long side of the box as shown. Cut slits in either side of the box as shown and thread your belt through these.

4 Cut a slit in the back of the box to fit the dagger blade in. Tape or glue the folded end of the dagger inside the box.

5 Now you are ready to get dressed. Wear the belt around your chest, with the box and dagger on your back. Wrap a sheet around your waist and put it over your shoulder. Arrange it so that it disguises the box but you can see the dagger poking out.

Next time, listen!

✱ Caesar was repeatedly warned of danger and eventually on the day somebody handed him a note all about the plot to kill him. He put it on his pile of work to read later. Doh!

✱ Caesar was stabbed 23 times. No need to make that many daggers, though.

✱ Caesar had a horrible hairstyle. Embarrassed by his baldness he brushed his remaining straggly hairs forward over his head, as if that ever fooled anyone ever.

WARNING! EXTRA-DISGUSTING ZONE!

OH, MUMMY!

The ancient Egyptians had a seriously yucky specialty. They were experts at preserving dead bodies as mummies, just in case the dead person might need a body in the afterlife.

Famous mummy Pharaoh Tutankhamen may have died from gangrene (a stinking flesh-rotting infection) after he broke his leg.

How to make a mummy

To be a mummy maker, you had to be a **top priest**.
Here are your step-by-step instructions:

1. Cut the body open with your sacred sharp stone. Take out the lungs, stomach, and other gooey organs. Put them in jars to bury near the body.

2. Knock a hole in the nose bone using a hammer and chisel. Hook the brain out and scrape out any extra parts with a long spoon.

3. Stuff the body and cover it with a salty preserving mixture. Leave it for a month or so (keep it guarded in case animals get to it. It smells tasty to them). Then wrap it up in resin-soaked bandages while saying lots of spells.

Not so fast, mummy

Once a mummy was in its tomb, the soul had to go on a treacherous journey to the ancient Egyptian version of heaven. It had to travel by boat along the river of death, go through a doorway guarded by serpents, and then wait while the god **Anubis** weighed its **heart** on some weighing scales against the "**feather of truth**." If the scales didn't balance, all that careful mummifying would be wasted. The dead person would get eaten by a monster that was part lion, part crocodile, and part hippo.

❖ Mummies would have one big problem in the afterlife— no brain. Ancient Egyptians thought the brain wasn't important, so the mummifiers took it out and threw it away.

❖ Coffins were often recycled, in other words, taken out of tombs and used again for other bodies.

❖ The Chinchorro people of Chile were making mummies long before the Egyptians. They cut bodies up and attached the pieces together again with sticks before coating them in mud.

Dying to get in

Ancient Egyptians wrote curses on the walls of tombs to scare away grave robbers looking for treasure. Despite this, many tombs were robbed, even though thieves risked being tortured to death.

° Two paper towel rolls
° Aluminum foil
° Cream or darker brown colored masking tape
° Wax crayons
° One cat (only kidding there, folks)

TUTEN-CAT-MUN

The ancient Egyptians thought cats were lucky. So they mummified them! Here's how to make your own lucky Egyptian mummified cat to display in your lovely home.

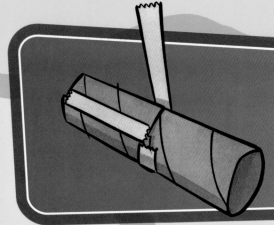

1 Cut a paper towel roll in half lenghtways, and wrap it over the other one. Tape it in place and flatten the rolls a little.

2 Model a simple cat head shape in foil, with a long neck you can stick into the paper towel rolls. Tape it in place. Stuff a small ball of foil in the bottom, too.

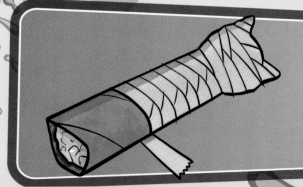

3 Wrap strips of masking tape around and around the head and paper towel rolls.

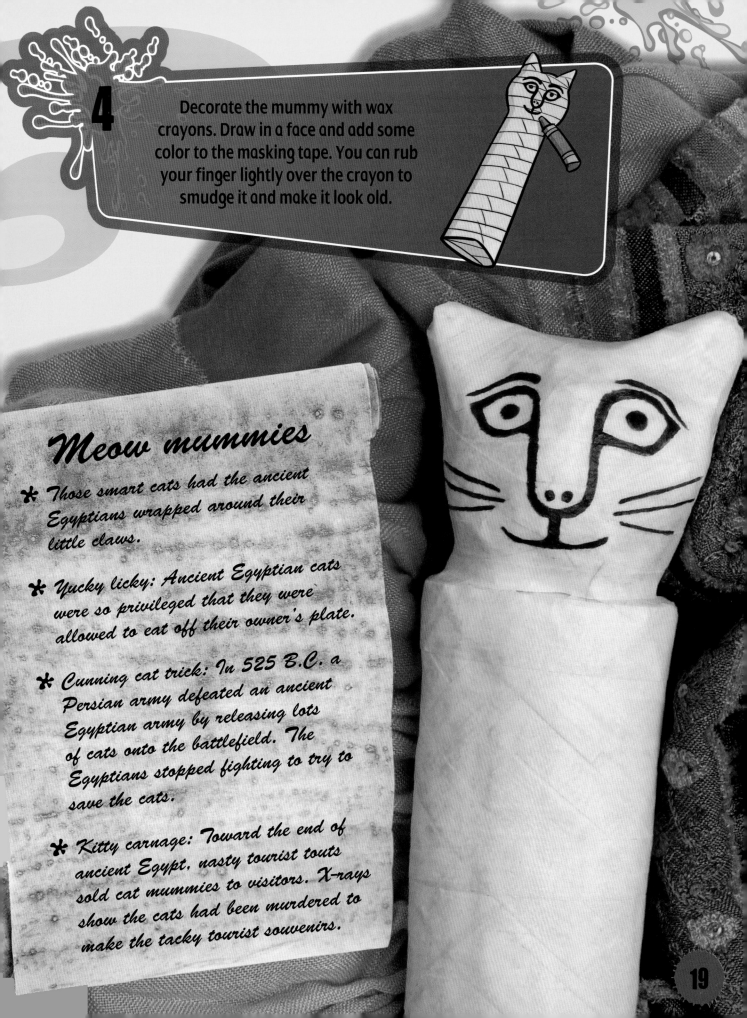

4 Decorate the mummy with wax crayons. Draw in a face and add some color to the masking tape. You can rub your finger lightly over the crayon to smudge it and make it look old.

Meow mummies

* Those smart cats had the ancient Egyptians wrapped around their little claws.

* Yucky licky: Ancient Egyptian cats were so privileged that they were allowed to eat off their owner's plate.

* Cunning cat trick: In 525 B.C. a Persian army defeated an ancient Egyptian army by releasing lots of cats onto the battlefield. The Egyptians stopped fighting to try to save the cats.

* Kitty carnage: Toward the end of ancient Egypt, nasty tourist touts sold cat mummies to visitors. X-rays show the cats had been murdered to make the tacky tourist souvenirs.

CRUMMY CASTLES

Could you poop out of a hole in a wall, sleep on a pile of stinky straw, and dodge the flaming arrows of besiegers on a regular basis? If so, you'd be really comfortable in a medieval castle.

Knock! Knock! Knights outside!

The defenders inside a besieged castle might be pelted with flaming arrows, rocks, and even rotting dead animals fired from trebuchets, which were **giant wooden catapults**.

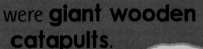

Joust!

Calling all brave knights. A joust will be held at the castle next week. Good prizes!*

❖ Lords held regular jousting competitions for knights at their castles, but it was a dangerous sport.

❖ A sure way to suffer was to get trapped falling from a horse, and then get dragged along horribly under the hooves.

❖ Amputation was common after jousts or battles. The limb had to be cut off as quickly as possible with a sword or saw, and the stump burned on the end with something very hot to seal it up.

❖ The crowd wasn't always safe. Occasionally wooden spectator stands collapsed.

*Only knights with life insurance allowed to enter. The lord of the castle cannot be held responsible for eyes being poked out, arms being chopped off, or armor scratches.

In 1203, French **knights** got inside a besieged castle by **crawling up a sewage trench**, disguised as locals. Once inside, the stinky besiegers lowered the drawbridge for their friends.

I'd rather be eating hay.

Doo-doo digger

If you were a servant in a **castle**, you would serve the lord who lived there. Hopefully you wouldn't get the job of "gong farmer" ("gong" meant "poop"). There were no toilets, so people **pooped** out of **holes in the wall** or down long chutes to the ground. It was the gong farmer's job to clear up the mess.

Don't fall off!

In the late 1400s, armor got so heavy that knights couldn't get up off of the ground once they had fallen off a horse.

PIRATES AHOY!

The most famous pirate captains roamed the seas off the Americas during a time called "The Golden Age" in the early 1700s. They were the type of pirates who waved cutlasses and hoisted scary flags.

Surrender! We want to party!

Pirates tried to scare their enemies with threats and make them surrender without a battle. Once they caught a ship, they would force the crew to become pirates, too, or face death. Then they would return to their hideouts, such as the pirate island of Tortuga in the Caribbean, where they would quickly spend all the treasure they had won by partying the night away.

WANTED!

Here is a foul foursome of the most disgustingly behaved pirate rogues ever to sail the high seas:

Edward Low
One of the most cruel pirates ever. He is said to have once cut off and cooked a man's lips.

Henry Morgan
Accidentally blew up his own ship during a party, killing 350 men but escaping himself.

Blackbeard
Went into battle with burning fuses tied in his hair to make him look devilish. He drank rum mixed with gunpowder.

William Kidd
After he was caught his corpse was left hanging in a cage to rot for 43 years. He knew it was going to happen because they measured him for his chains while he was still alive.

Deadly dancing

When pirates got caught by the authorities, they could expect a nasty punishment. Whole crews were sometimes hanged together in public. In England, the most notorious pirates were hanged and then their bodies were covered in tar and hung publicly in an **iron cage**, where they slowly rotted away.

Pirate flags were designed to scare people, sending the message "surrender quickly or die."

If pirates ever caught a **naval officer**, they would find out how he had treated his men. If he had been cruel, he'd be doomed to the same treatment!

- A friendly adult to help you with the oven steps
- A foil-lined baking sheet
- Bowl and tablespoon
- 4 heaping tablespoons all-purpose flour
- 1 tablespoon salt
- 3 tablespoons water
- Paint and paintbrush
- White craft glue
- Black felt
- Scissors
- Oven mitts

SEA-DOG SOUVENIRS

Make a false eye, finger bones and a piece of Blackbeard's beard. Then bring out these priceless and satisfyingly sick fake pirate treasures to astound your friends. You could make up a story about how your ancestor chopped off Blackbeard's finger, stole his eye, and pulled off some of his beard during a fight.

1 Heat up an oven to 275°F. Mix up the flour, salt, and water to make a soft dough.

2 Roll a round eye about the size of a walnut. Roll a small hotdog to make a finger bone—fat on the ends and thin in the middle. Finger bones are about 1 ½ inches long.

3 Put the models on the baking sheet. Bake the finger bone for about two hours, and the eye for about three hours. They should be hard when done. Use oven mitts for this stage.

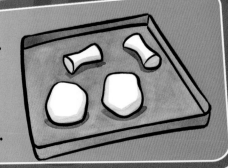

4

When cooled, paint both models white. Then, when the white is dry, add more detailing. Finally, coat your models with white craft glue, which will dry clear.

5

To make a piece of Blackbeard's beard, soak the felt in warm soapy water and pull it around until it can be torn. Pull around the edges to make it straggly!

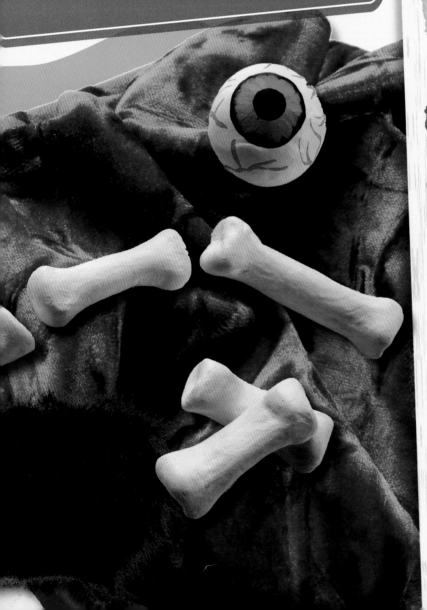

Don't upset a pirate

Here are some horrible pirate punishments. Surely Blackbeard would have done the same to you if you'd ever tried to pull off his beard.

✱ **Keelhauling:** A sailor was dragged on a rope underwater, from one side of a ship to the other. He could drown or at least be slashed open by the razor-sharp barnacles on the ship's hull.

✱ **Marooning:** For cheating fellow pirates, a man would be left on a desert island (often just a sandbar), with a little food, water, and a loaded pistol to kill himself.

✱ **Flogging:** A man was tied to a mast and then had his bare back lashed with thick knotted ropes.

✱ **Walking the plank:** Although a famous pirate punishment, this is probably a myth!

ROYAL NUTCASES

Down the centuries many kings and queens have been insane, smelly, and downright disgusting.

No wonder Louis XIV of France had only two baths ever. In his 2,000-room palace at Versailles near Paris, there were no bathrooms.

Your Royal Smelliness

Like lots of people in history, monarchs mostly stank. For instance, English king **Henry VIII** had a "**groom of the stool**," a nobleman responsible for cleaning his toilet and wiping his bum for him (and there was no toilet paper). Henry also had six wives—and had two of them executed. Oh, and by the time he died at the age of 55, he was covered in boils and so overweight that he couldn't move around by himself.

However much they're paying me to do this job, it isn't enough.

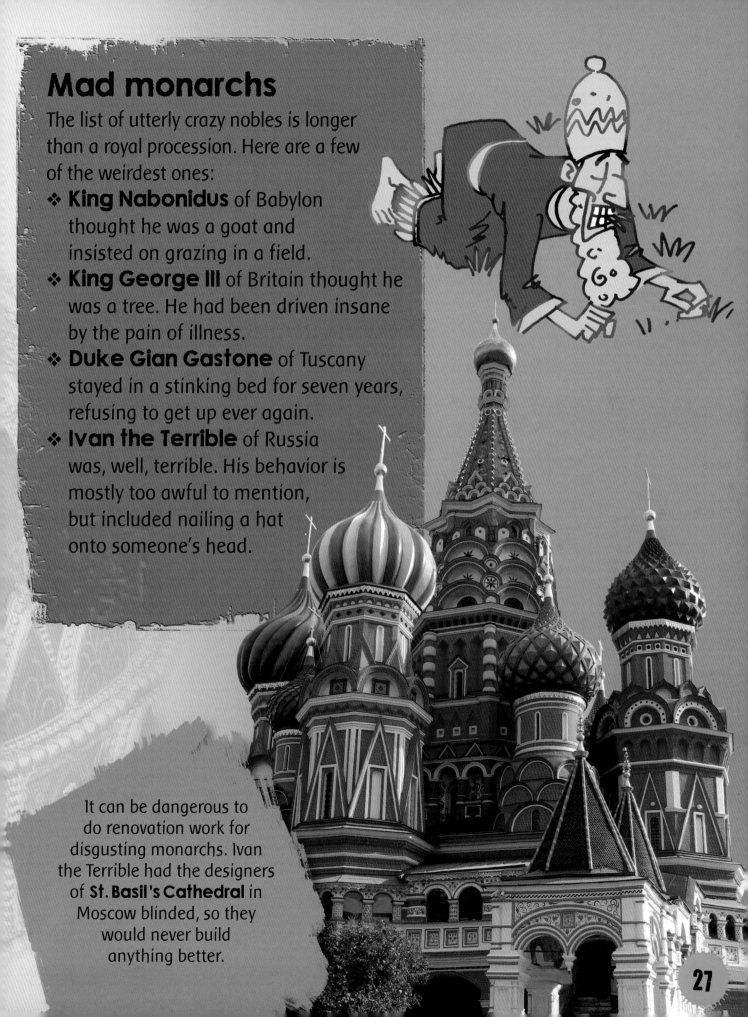

Mad monarchs

The list of utterly crazy nobles is longer than a royal procession. Here are a few of the weirdest ones:

❖ **King Nabonidus** of Babylon thought he was a goat and insisted on grazing in a field.

❖ **King George III** of Britain thought he was a tree. He had been driven insane by the pain of illness.

❖ **Duke Gian Gastone** of Tuscany stayed in a stinking bed for seven years, refusing to get up ever again.

❖ **Ivan the Terrible** of Russia was, well, terrible. His behavior is mostly too awful to mention, but included nailing a hat onto someone's head.

It can be dangerous to do renovation work for disgusting monarchs. Ivan the Terrible had the designers of **St. Basil's Cathedral** in Moscow blinded, so they would never build anything better.

27

DOCTOR, THAT'S DISGUSTING!

Getting sick is never any fun, but in days gone by the medical cures were often more dangerous than the illness.

Humor her

For centuries, people believed the world was made of four important parts, called "humors." These were fire, air, earth, and water—in the body, these were represented by yellow bile, blood, black bile, and phlegm.* It was thought that people got sick if there was too much of one or other humor in the body.

* Phlegm is what you probably call snot. Bile is stomach juices.

Dreadful doctors

Roman writer Pliny suggested a good inscription for a Roman tombstone: "It was the doctors that killed me."

R.I.P
I BLAME THE DOCTOR

Take one a day (if you dare)

Here are some sickening medical prescriptions from history:

❖ Ancient Egyptian baldness cure: Rub crocodile fat and lettuce leaves on your head.

❖ Roman cure for a stomach upset: Gargle with mustard.

❖ Medieval cure for a fit: Sniff crumbs of roasted cuckoo up your nose.

❖ Medieval cure for a fever (left): Eat a spider wrapped in a raisin.

Bad blood

A common treatment in history was bloodletting, which means getting rid of some blood. This was a disastrous idea that often made the patient weaker. Bloodletting was done by cutting or by attaching **leeches**, animals that look like fat black worms, to the patient's skin. They would hook onto the skin, **suck blood**, and then drop off when they were full.

Medieval medical men thought they could tell a lot from a patient's urine (pee). These weird pee watchers liked to examine it when it was fresh and warm. They smelled it or even **drank a little** to taste it.

Stinky Stupid Fashion

Fashion in history often made people look totally stupid, added to their general smelliness, and sometimes even helped to kill them.

Big bums

In the 1800s, women wore "**bustles,**" bum-padding that made them look as if they had a behind with a big shelf on top.

Hot stuff

No wonder people were always fighting in medieval Europe. They must have been driven mad by their itchy, hot, woolen clothing, worn even in summer. Only the very rich could afford something that didn't give them heat rash. Everyone else must have smelled like damp blankets. Things got even hotter in the 1700s, when wealthy people wore **heavy wigs** made from goat, horse, or human hair (collected from poor or dead people).

I wish I'd talked this plan over with my family before I did it.

Filthy Fashion Facts

❖ In the 1100s, there was a fashion for shoes with really long, curly toes. They were called "pikasese" because they had a pointed end, like a "pike."

❖ In medieval castles, clothes were stored near where people pooped because the smell drove away moths, which nibble holes in clothing.

❖ In the 1600s, men and women wore white makeup made of poisonous white lead mixed with vinegar. It shriveled and rotted their skin.

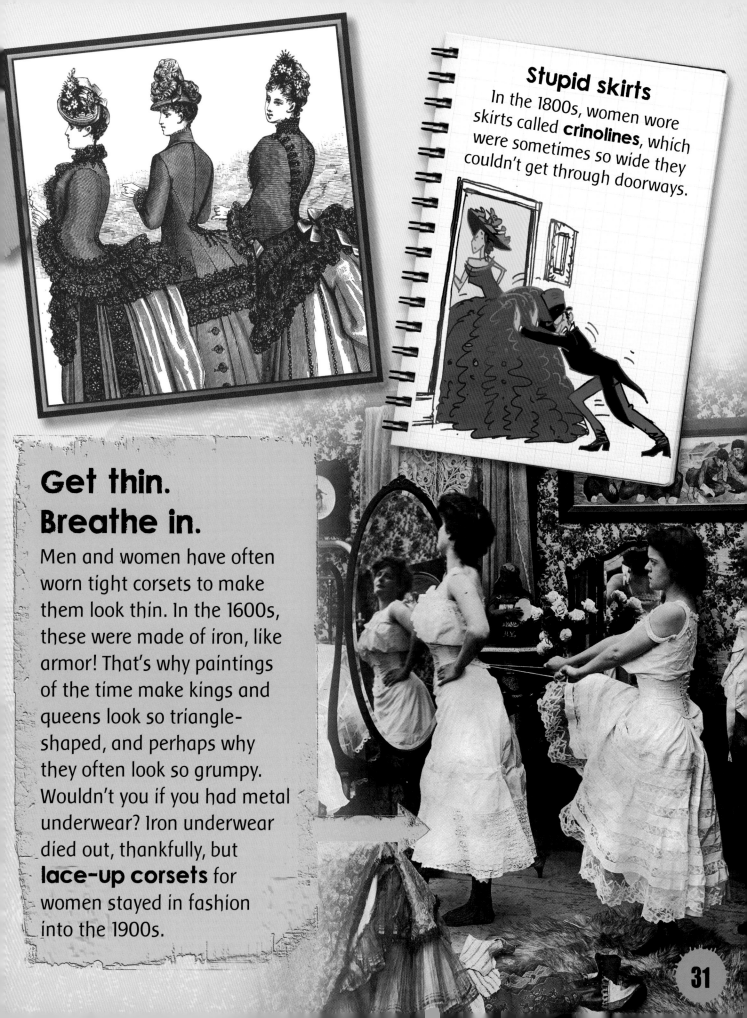

Stupid skirts

In the 1800s, women wore skirts called **crinolines**, which were sometimes so wide they couldn't get through doorways.

Get thin.
Breathe in.

Men and women have often worn tight corsets to make them look thin. In the 1600s, these were made of iron, like armor! That's why paintings of the time make kings and queens look so triangle-shaped, and perhaps why they often look so grumpy. Wouldn't you if you had metal underwear? Iron underwear died out, thankfully, but **lace-up corsets** for women stayed in fashion into the 1900s.

WHO'D WANT TO BE A KID?

If there was a revolting, smelly, yucky job to do in history, kids usually got it. Going to school could be awful, too, and even babies got a raw deal.

Lucky you

Up until recent times it was considered normal for a teacher to **beat a child** in school.

If you thought school was bad...

The worst school ever has to have been in **Sparta**, now part of Greece, around **500 B.C.** Seven-year-old boys were sent away to military school to toughen them up for fighting. They slept on beds made of sharp reeds to get them used to pain. Lessons included staying silent while being whipped, and hunting and killing slaves.

Worst jobs for kids

For centuries kids from poor families had to work as soon as they could walk. It was especially bad in the 1800s, when many new industries started up. Children five years of age were forced up **chimneys** to clean them. Six year olds were attached to coal carts and made to crawl around mine tunnels, while match girls worked 12-hour shifts making matches using deadly, poisonous phosphorus. The conditions for these poor children really *were* disgusting.

One of the worst jobs for kids in the 1800s was collecting dog and cat poop from the ground to be used in making leather.

Oh, baby

With these chilling childcare treatments it's amazing anyone survived history.

❖ Roman fathers were shown their newborn babies and could choose whether the baby lived or died.

❖ Babies in history were often "swaddled"—so tightly wrapped in bandages they couldn't move.

❖ In medieval times, women fed their babies food they had already chewed themselves to make it mushy.

Sickening Science

YUCKY SCIENTISTS

We salute the world's inventors and scientists, geniuses who have done lots of dangerous gooey horrible experiments—so we don't have to!

C. F. Schönbein discovered "guncotton," used in firearms, when he spilt acid and mopped it up with his wife's apron. Later that day the apron exploded.

Sick way to cure sickness

In 1796, English scientist **Edward Jenner** discovered how to protect people against the fatal disease smallpox by injecting them with cowpox, a mild version of the disease. You might feel pretty sick yourself after reading what he did. He **collected pus** (the yellow goo you get in pimples) from the skin blisters of someone who had cowpox. He injected the pus into an eight-year-old boy and then injected him with smallpox to see if he would catch it. The boy was fine and Jenner became famous for finding a vaccine.

I always knew scientists were crackers, but this takes the cake.

36

Brush off those bacteria

In 1676, microscope-maker Antonie van Leeuwenhoek was the first person to discover bacteria. He studied his own plaque (the yellow gunk that builds up on unbrushed teeth), and said that he saw "many very little living animalcules, very prettily a-moving."

Calling all scientists!
Forget inventing dull boring stuff for grown-ups. How about inventing instead:

❖ Self-cleaning bedrooms—No more moldy old plates, smelly socks, or dust piles on the floor, and no more nagging about tidying up!

❖ Parent calmer—To stop those tense grown-ups from getting all worked up about unimportant mess.

❖ Smell ray—For zapping your enemies with foot cheese or dog breath.

❖ Invisible nose—For secret picking.

Scientists make bad neighbors

You wouldn't want to live next door to famous artist and inventor **Leonardo da Vinci**, who lived in the 1400s. He liked to cut up dead humans and dead horses to see how they worked.

THE DISGUSTING SCIENCE AWARDS

Some inventions (and inventors) are just so nutty and yucky we think they deserve an award for their sick genius.

RIP

Here lie the facts about some scientists and inventors who experimented once too often...

❖ **Franz Reichelt. Died 1912.** The inventor of a combined overcoat and parachute, he tested his invention by jumping off the Eiffel Tower in Paris. It didn't work.

❖ **Alexander Bogdanov. Died 1928.** Convinced that blood transfusions could make people young again, he fatally gave himself the blood of someone infected with the deadly diseases malaria and tuberculosis.

❖ **Thomas Midgley. Died 1944.** Midgley accidentally strangled himself on his patent pulley-operated mechanical bed.

Award for Smell Science

Scientists in Japan have invented a smell recorder, a machine that can "record" and "play back" a smell, using a mix of chemicals to copy what it smelled. This would be a great present for those who might want to store a memory of their best farts. But if you find farting embarrassing, "**farty pants" underwear** has also been invented, with a smell-absorbing pad to catch those stinkers.

The **Horrible Invention Award** goes to American George Hogan, who designed an alarm clock that tipped water down people's necks to wake them up.

The **Pee Science Award** goes to scientists in Singapore for creating a **pee-powered battery**. It has a little slit where you can pop in a drop of pee to make an electrical charge inside the battery.

Award for Poop Science

Scientists at the University of Washington receive lots of poop in the mail, because park rangers in Africa send them elephant dung to analyze for DNA. That way the scientists can create a poop-inspired map of the elephant population across Africa.

Stinky Science

Smells are everywhere, not just in your stinky socks. So why is the world such a smelly place?

Worst whiff

American chemists have invented the world's worst smell. They call it "**stench soup**," and they created it to use as a stink weapon. After lots of practicing, the nose-nobbling chemists found the best formula was a mix of chemicals that smelled like a combination of vomit, rotting flesh, and sweet fruit. Stench soup smells so ghastly that people run away from it.

Smelly joke

If your nose runs and your feet smell, you were probably made upside-down!

40

Bad Smellometer

Here's a list of smells that we find really gross. They're all created by really minging chemical molecules.

Skunk spray
A stinky splatter a skunk can spray more than 20 feet.

Rotten fish
Your brain will signal to you not to eat rotting fish. Listen to your brain!

Pet poop
Not only stinky but also a nasty squelchy surprise on the bottom of your shoe.

Dirty dishcloth
Bacteria on dirty dishcloths make them smell terrible. They're also a health hazard.

Old potato peel
Slimy rotting vegetables smell like the soup mix from hell.

The farting farm

Ever wondered why farms are so smelly? Smells are made of tiny building blocks called molecules. Down on the farm, **cows and pigs** make lots of stinky gases by farting, pooping, or belching. The stink molecules attach themselves to dust particles in the air (farms have a lot of dust). Then the smell gets blown over to the neighbors along with the dust.

Cheese, anyone?
Ammonia is a common stinky chemical. You'll smell ammonia around uncleaned toilets and **ripe cheeses**, such as camembert.

What you need →

° Some small raisins (which look really like rabbit poop)

° A glass jar, tumbler, or bottle

° Carbonated water

° Thin colored cardboard, or plain cardboard and felt-tip pen or paint

EAT UP, BUNNY!

This easy experiment cleverly demonstrates not one, but two, important scientific pieces of information. It shows how bubbles of gas behave, and it represents how rabbits eat their own poop. It's ideal for this vile book, don't you think?

1 Decorate a strip of cardboard with a picture of a bunny bending down with his tongue out and his tail in the air.

The bunny sits on the bottom edge of the cardboard.

Wrap the cardboard around the container, taping it securely so that it will sit high up with plenty of water showing beneath.

2

3 Fill the container with the carbonated water. Drop the raisins in. The raisins sink at first, then start to go up and down, up and down for ages, as if by magic. It will look as if your bunny is pooping them and eating them, just like his furry cousins do in the beautiful outdoors.

If you don't want to go to the trouble of making the cardboard, just say the raisins are poop you've collected from a magic bunny who spoke to you in the yard.

WHY DOES BUNNY DO THAT?

AS A SHARP-BRAINED SCIENTIST, YOU'LL WANT TO KNOW "WHY?" NOT, "WHY WOULD I EVER WANT TO DO THIS DISGUSTING THING?" BUT, "WHY DOES THIS AMAZING RAISIN/BUNNY POOP DISPLAY WORK?" GLAD YOU ASKED!

1. CARBONATED WATER CONTAINS A GAS CALLED CO_2, IT MAKES BUBBLES IN THE LIQUID.

2. THE BUBBLES OF GAS COLLECT ON THE RAISINS (YOU CAN SEE THIS HAPPENING). GAS IS REALLY LIGHT COMPARED TO LIQUID, SO THE BUBBLES FLOAT UP LIKE TINY BALLOONS, LIFTING THE RAISINS.

3. WHEN THE RAISINS GET TO THE SURFACE, THE BUBBLES POP AND THE GAS FLOATS AWAY. THE RAISINS SINK AND THE WHOLE THING STARTS AGAIN.

Before You Swallow...

...do you *really* know what goes into the food you eat?

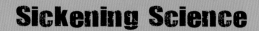

Fish sundae
Indian food scientists have developed an extra-healthy low-fat **ice cream**—made using cooked **cuttlefish**.

Bad bacteria

Bacteria want your food! They are microscopic living things that live just about everywhere on the planet and they spend their whole time feeding. Most bacteria are harmless, but nasty ones can make food rot and will make you sick if you accidentally eat them. If food is going bad, that means more and more **bacteria** will be **crawling** over it. A piece of chicken that is beginning to smell off will be covered with about 60 million bacteria per square inch!

Ingredients: You'd be surprised!

Some chemicals added to foods have other useful, but not so tasty, jobs:

Titanium dioxide
Used as food coloring in salad dressings, but also in sunscreen and paint!

Sodium phosphate
Used in packaged meals to stop the food ingredients from separating, but also used in soap.

Propylene glycol
Used in lime- or orange-flavored foods and also used to poison beetles, make deodorant, and to cool down car engines.

Mom's excelled herself this time!

Flavors can be copied using chemicals. If "chocolate-flavored" is on a product, it probably means it doesn't actually have any chocolate in it.

What is that stuff?

On food labels, you'll often see a list of chemicals that have been added to make the product last and taste good. Here's the lowdown:

Coloring: Without coloring, canned foods, such as peas, would be a sludgy brown color.

Stabilizers: Stabilizers keep a food from going crumbly. They are often made from seaweed, but one type of stabilizer—xanthum gum—is a colorless slime made by a type of bacteria fed on sugar.

Preservatives: Without these chemicals, food would soon rot or become infested with crunchy creepy-crawlies, such as mites or maggots.

Anticaking agent: Not a dieting secret agent, but a chemical that stops powdered food from going lumpy.

Emulsifiers: These chemicals stop products, such as mayonnaise, from separating out into an oily mess.

HELLISH VACATIONS

Would you like to visit another planet in our solar system? Read this first, before you book the journey to hell!

Mom, are we there yet?

Fry or freeze

The solar system is made up of all the planets that travel around the Sun. The "inner planets," the ones nearest the Sun, are Mercury, Venus, Mars, and Earth. Mercury is desolate and rocky, with no air to breathe. Half the planet is boiling hot, while the other half is unimaginably cold. Meanwhile, Venus has 220-mile-per-hour winds, a permanent smog that traps heat close to the ground and a surface temperature of 540°F, while Mars has an atmosphere of choking gas, plus massive dust storms. There's definitely nowhere to put up a deck chair on any of the inner planets, except Earth.

When is the Moon heaviest?

When it's full.

Stinky gas balls

If you traveled out to Jupiter, Saturn, Uranus, or Neptune, you'd find giant balls of foul stinking gases, including methane and ammonia—the gases that make sewage smell so bad. The surfaces of these super-smelly planets are thought to be deadly liquid gas oceans, and huge lightning storms go on all the time. Don't expect any hotels.

Space junk

There are more than a million pieces of man-made space junk orbiting Earth. If you're unlucky, one could smash into your spaceship.

What to expect when on vacation in space

All the other planets are very far away from Earth, and most would take years to reach. Scientists have worked out what might be the dangers of traveling for many years in space.

❖ **Getting sick**—Some medicines have been found not to work so well in space. It would definitely be no fun to get diarrhea in a spacesuit.

❖ **Going insane**—Imagine being cooped up in a spaceship with the same people for most of your life! It'd be even worse than going on vacation with your family.

❖ **Weighing more**—On planets bigger than Earth, gravity is stronger, which means you'd be heavier. Getting on the weighing scales would be a big shock.

Matter Splatters

- 1 cup grated cheese (use a hard cheese that melts well, such as cheddar or parmesan)
- Baking sheet, lined with foil, parchment paper, or a nonstick sheet to stop the cheese from sticking
- Oven mitts
- A watch with a second hand, or a digital watch
- A friendly adult to help you with the hot stuff

Remember, we said everything is made up of little molecules? Well, we did, so concentrate. Here's how to alter some molecules yourself—and end up with some tasty cheese splatters along the way!

1 Heat an oven to 375°F. Make little piles of cheese on the baking sheet. The bigger the piles, the bigger your splats will be.

2 Put the sheet in the oven. Use oven mitts to open the oven and keep a watch on it every minute (because cheese melts quickly and could burn). It should take about 6 minutes to melt.

3 Use oven mitts to take the sheet out when the melted splatters look golden, but before they burn.

4 Let the splatters cool down. Then peel them off the sheet and eat them.

You're a scientific genius!

If you made splatters, then you altered matter!

Here's how.

✱ Cheese contains lots of fat molecules. They loosen up and turn soft when they are heated.

✱ Cheese contains a type of molecule called casein protein. These proteins are normally bundled up in tight coils.

✱ When the protein molecules get hot, they uncoil and tangle up with each other.

✱ Cheese also contains molecules of liquid that evaporate (float away) when it is heated. When the melted cheese dries out, it has much less liquid, so it turns crispy

Take that, Einstein!

THE SCIENCE OF POOP

Everybody poops. Hopefully they poop in the toilet. But what happens to it then? Sewage science comes to the rescue to stop our number twos from becoming our number one problem.*

Poop more, grow more

Humanure is the name given to sewage that has been recycled to make farm fertilizer. Then people eat the crops, poop them out, and the whole cycle starts again. Just beautiful, don't you think?

*Find out more solid facts on poop on page 67! After all, this kind of stinky stuff is why you bought the book, isn't it?

Another drink?

When you flush, the "effluent" (poop and pee) goes into the sewage system. It goes through pipes and pumping stations to a **sewage treatment works**. Here, liquid and solids are separated and treated to make them safe. Tiny creatures called microorganisms help remove dangerous substances. Eventually the liquid becomes clean water. It goes back into rivers. Poop becomes sludge, a harmless muddy mixture. It is put in landfills or turned into fertilizer.

Filthy Facts

We've flushed out some fascinating facts:

❖ The average person visits the toilet 2,500 times a year.

❖ The first toilet stall in a public restroom is likely to be the cleanest because it is the least used.

❖ To find out more about toilets, visit the Sulabh International Museum of Toilets in New Delhi, India.

❖ Until 1858, raw sewage ran down the streets of **London**. Then they had a hot summer... The awful smell became known as the **Great Stink**. After that the government built proper sewers.

Some people don't bother with sewage works, and instead pump raw sewage out into the sea.

Eco-poop

If you use an eco-friendly **composting toilet**, you can sit safe in the knowledge that your poop is helping humankind. This type of toilet has its own colony of microorganisms that work away underneath the toilet, breaking down sewage into harmless compost, which helps fertilize the ground. This way your number twos become little eco-warriors, helping to reduce pollution.

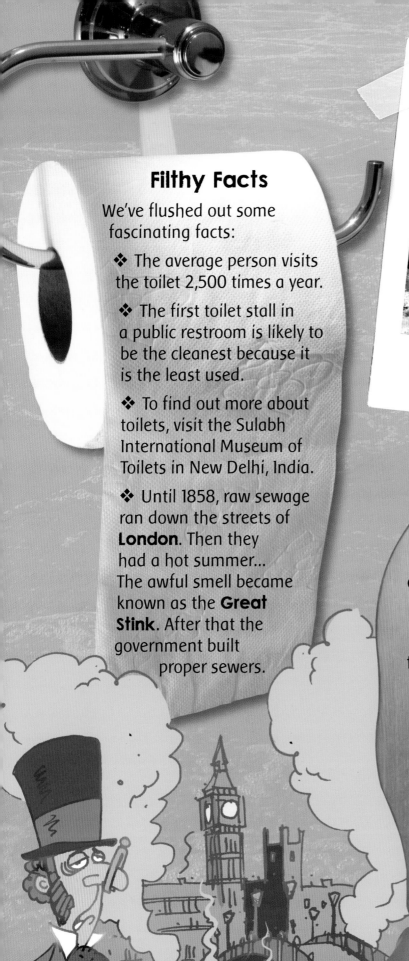

ROTTEN ROBOTS

Robots are friendly…
Or ARE they?

Top toilet robots

❖ Computer geeks have designed an automatic **robot toilet flusher** using Lego, called Roboflush. It says "Thank you," then flushes when someone gets off the toilet or puts the lid down.

❖ Look out for Dasubee the urinal elephant if you ever visit Kobe Airport in Japan. It's a robot that can scrub a toilet in 10 seconds, saving a lot of water. It's shaped like a big blue elephant and has a cute little yellow hat.

❖ A robot toilet at Frankfurt Airport in Germany has its own robot arm that extends and sprays water at the toilet bowl.

Attack of the gray goo

Nanotechnology is going to be one of the next big steps in science. It's the idea of creating incredibly small robots from just a teeny-tiny molecule or two to do all kinds of jobs. But some people have warned that dangerous nanorobots could be made that might start to replicate (make new versions of themselves). This might be so hard to stop they cover the world in **gray goo**!

Robot rudeness

Humanoid robots are built to look and behave like humans. For instance, the "robosapien" robot toy (below) can even make farting and belching noises. The most convincing humanoid robot head is K-Bot, built in the U.S. It has fake skin and lots of computer software and tiny motors inside to make different facial expressions. Cameras behind its eyes study the face of anyone looking at it, and then it copies the expression it sees. It can sneer or squint just like a bad-mannered human!

There are robots designed to play in robot soccer teams, fight each other, or do housework.

A U.S. university has built a "**nanocar**," a nanorobot made of a tiny molecule, with even smaller round molecules as wheels.

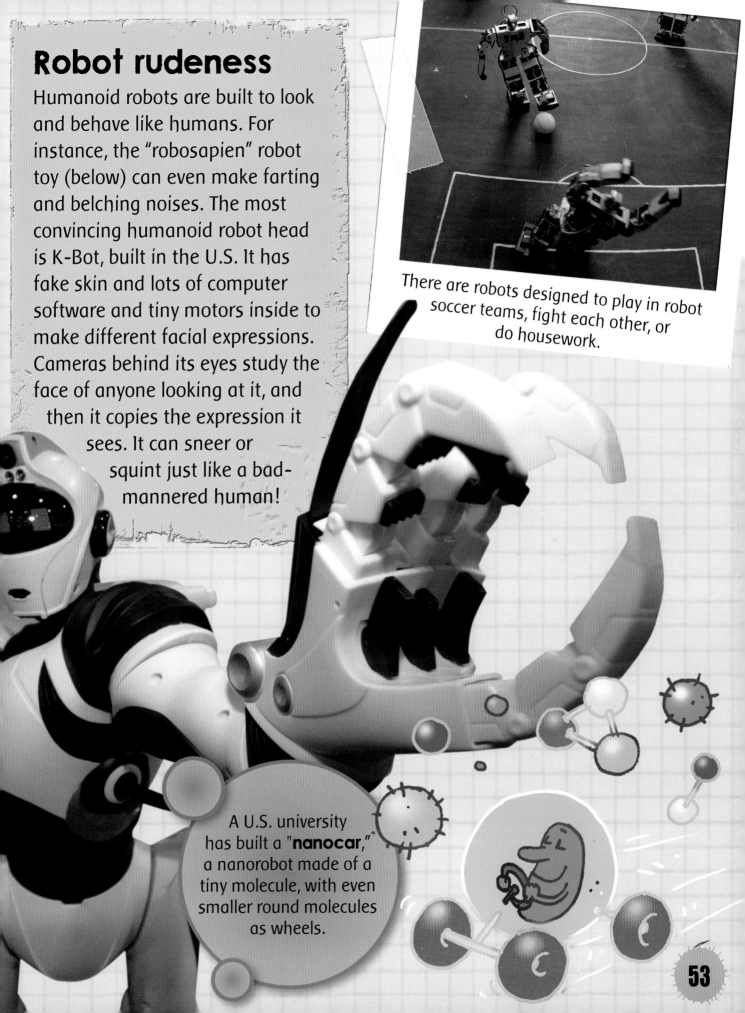

- Thick rigid cardboard (such as a shoebox)
- Scissors
- Ruler
- Tape or glue
- Crayons, paint, or colored paper for decorating Bigmouth

BIGMOUTHED ROBOT

Here's how to create your own robot to do your dirty work for you. He works perfectly for those times when you really want to say something awful, but wouldn't dare. No probs. He'll do it for you!

1 Cut out a rectangular robot head about 11 inches x 7 ½ inches. Cut a square mouth about 2 ½ inches x 2 ½ inches, and save the piece.

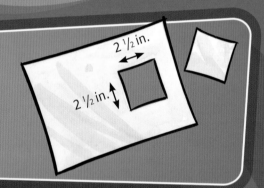

2 ½ in.

2 ½ in.

Paper or cardboard strip

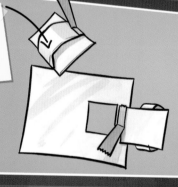

2 Cut out a piece of cardboard about 4 inches x 3 ½ inches, and tape a strip of cardboard to the back of it as shown. Then tape the big piece onto the head to make a neck.

3 Cut out a cardboard piece narrower than the neck but twice as long. Find the mouthpiece from step 1 and tape it onto the top (tape *over* the edges so that the pieces can flap apart).

4 Slide the mouth up through the sleeve at the back of the neck. Then hook it over the mouth. You can then pull it up and down to make the robot "shout." Decorate your robot however you like. Draw a robot-style face on him, paint him, or glue colored paper on him. Slanting eyebrows will make him look angry.

If you want, cut a hole for your finger.

Things robots say

Bigmouthed robot should say only what you want him to, but, like most movie or TV robots, he may go mad and want to take over the world. Avoid him if he starts saying "You must be exterminated," or "I'm in charge."

How to be a Weirdo

Are you tired of looking like everybody else? Do you fancy growing an extra ear, or maybe glowing in the dark so you don't need a bedside light anymore? Medical science can help you become the kookiest-looking weirdo on the block.

How to glow in the dark

Every cell of every living thing has DNA inside it. DNA is a kind of chemical code that tells a cell to do something. So, for instance, a mouse has DNA in its cells that makes it grow whiskers and a tail. Scientists have worked out how to alter DNA, and that can lead to some weird mixtures. While testing DNA-altering techniques, scientists mixed mouse cells with green glow-in-the-dark DNA from a jellyfish, and ended up with **glowing mice**!

How to grow an extra ear

In 1997, U.S. scientists grew a **human-shaped ear** on the back of a **mouse**. They did this as an experiment to work out if they could grow replacement human ears. The ear could be safely removed from the mouse, without the mouse dying. Here's how they did it, step by step:

1. They bred a hairless mouse.

2. They made an ear-shaped framework on the mouse's back, using the material doctors use to make stitches that dissolve.

3. They put some cartilage cells from a cow's knee onto the frame. Cartilage is springy stuff that connects things together in the body. Ears are made from it.

4. The cells grew around the frame to make an ear shape.

Plastic surgery is having an operation to change your appearance. It can make you fatter or thinner, younger or older, or even change your skin color.

How to become a work of art

Australian artist Stelios Arcadious had an **ear implanted in his arm** to make him a living art exhibit. It was grown from cells in a laboratory.

It's Sick in Space!

Astronauts are certainly brave people. Who else would want to do a job where your bones waste away, you get sick, and you have to keep your underwear on for days? Space science isn't pleasant when it comes to humans.

Space toilets have bars like rollercoaster chairs to stop the spacemen from floating away as they do their space business.

Astronauts are wimps

Because they are weightless in space, astronauts turn into **weedy wimps**. They don't use their muscles as much as they would on Earth, so their muscles get weak and their bones start to weaken, too. They have to exercise for two hours a day to avoid getting too weak and wobbly, and, when they return home to Earth, it takes about three months to go back to normal.

Without a spacesuit in outer space, you would quickly suffocate from lack of air. Then the liquid inside your body would evaporate away, because there is no air pressure to keep it inside you. You would quickly turn into a frozen lump.

Barfing sneezing spacemen

Yucky things happen to astronauts. Here's a list of what they have to put up with:

Space sickness: This feels like car sickness, and it's caused by being weightless and floating around, not knowing which way is up and which way is down.

Space snot: Because there's no gravity pulling things down in space, the liquids inside the human body move upward toward the head. Astronauts feel as if they have a heavy cold. Their noses are filled with snot and their faces puff up.

Pee problem: Because of fluids moving upward in their body, astronauts feel as if they want to go to the toilet all the time. Eventually, however, they get used to it.

Filthy facts

❖ Blast Off! If you **farted in a spacesuit**, the smell would stay inside.

❖ Astronauts wear diapers during liftoff, reentry, and on spacewalks, all times when they can't get to a toilet.

❖ On the U.S. space shuttle, astronauts change their underwear every two days, and their clothes once every ten days.

❖ Before going into space, astronauts have to train on a special toilet simulator.

Space sucks

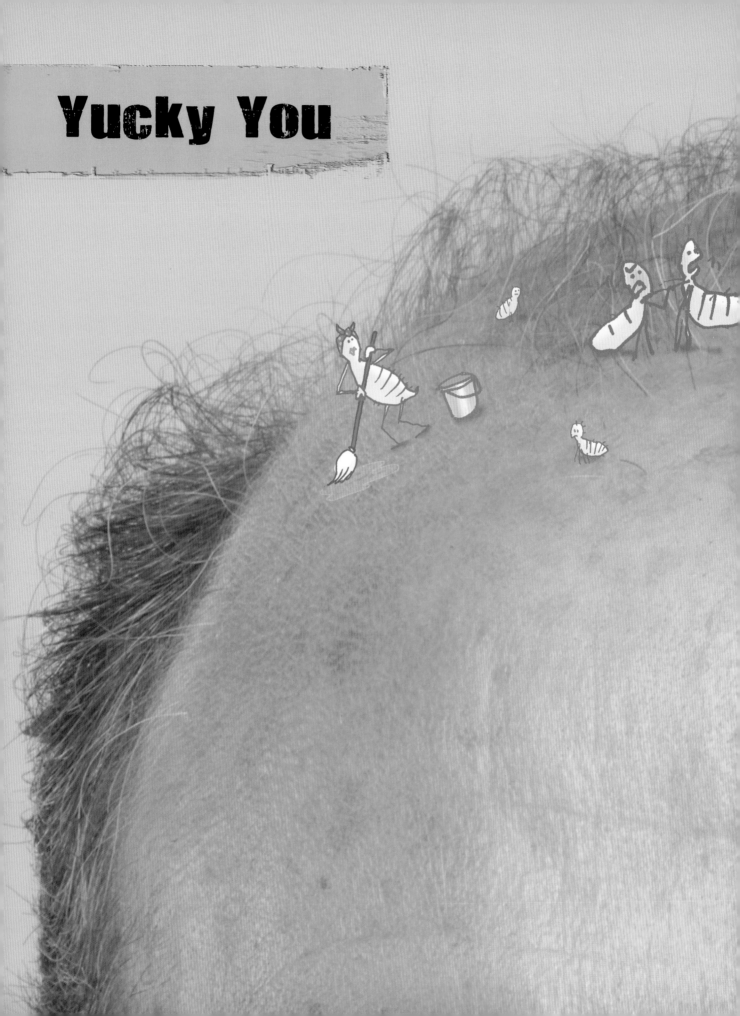

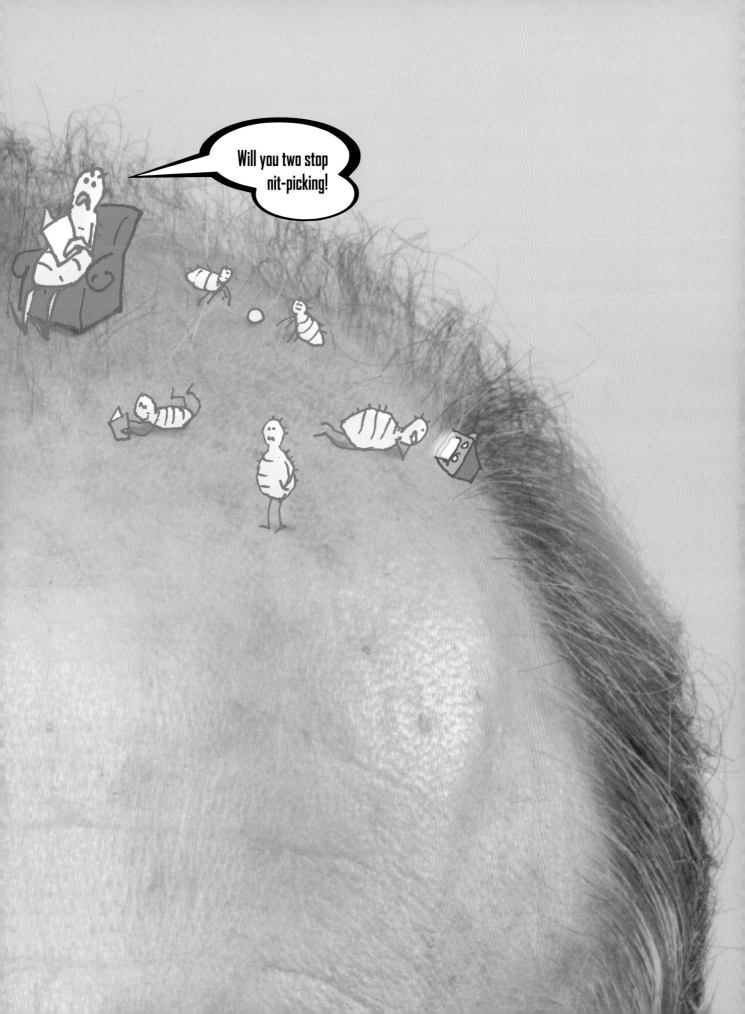

BOOGERS FOR BREAKFAST

What can you do if you're feeling hungry, but don't have a handy snack? Pick your nose and get chewing, of course! Here's why your nose gets so crusty.

Woo-hoo!

Snot swallower

When you breathe air in, you also breathe in other stuff such as dust, germs, and pollen. Some of these tiny parts can harm your lungs, so your nose is set up like a trap to catch them. Its main weapon is snot—runny goo with the proper name of mucus (pronounced mew-cus). This sticky nose lining traps the airborne particles. Then you swallow your snot and it slips down your throat into your stomach (unless you pick it out first, of course).

Filthy facts

❖ Scientists have a special name for nosepicking. It's called rhinotillexomania.

❖ A healthy person may swallow up to two cupfuls of snot a day. If you get a cold, though, your nose makes a lot more snot.

❖ In Basotho, South Africa, mothers keep their **babies' noses clean** by **sucking** the **snot** out.

What's the difference between green snot and broccoli?

Kids will eat snot.

SNEEZE ALERT!

If a big piece of dirt, pollen, or a germ gets stuck in among the hairs in your nose, you will automatically sneeze. **Aaaaa-choo!** A spray of snot, germs, and dirt hurtles out of your nose at up to 100 miles an hour. Anybody in the way will get spattered by your invisible germ-carrying mist, so cover your nose and mouth when you sneeze.

Let's go!

Perfect pickings

Snot is made of water, salt, dead body cells, and a kind of gluey sugary stuff called mucin. When the water dries out, the snot turns into hard boogers.

Time to infect some more people!

Why is snot green? Because it's snot blue! Actually, the color of the booger depends on the dirt, bacteria, or body cells it has floating in it.

- ¼ cup all-purpose flour
- 1 teaspoon water
- 1 tablespoon salt
- 2 tablespoons vegetable oil
- Washable green or yellow poster paint (if you want to smear this snot under your nose, use safety-tested green face paint)
- Bowl and spoon
- Box of strong tissues

'SNOT FUNNY

Here's how to make some fake snot to hide in a tissue. Fool your friends into thinking you sneezed it out. It's safe to smear on your fingers, too.

1 Put the flour and salt into the bowl and gradually mix in the oil.

Mix in enough water to make a slimy paste. **2**

3 Add enough paint to make a snot-green color (experiment to get the color you want).

4 Put some of the green slime in a tissue and hold it cupped in your hand. Pretend to sneeze into the tissue and then open it up. Look surprised when you see the slime! Or smear the snot under your nose or on your finger!

Practical Joke Tips

✱ Practical jokes work best if you pick somebody you know will laugh easily and won't mind the joke. So, for instance, a really strict teacher might not be pleased by your snot-covered hankie, but your friends will probably love it and want one of their own.

✱ Practical jokes work best if you practice them before you go out and perform in public. Work out what you are going to say during the trick, and keep it simple. Try saying something like "I think I've got a cold coming. A...aa...choo!"

Stomach It

Your stomach is like a busy factory, breaking down all the food you eat into ingredients your body can use. You can hear your stomach at work when it gurgles!

Vomit is half-digested food that comes back up from the stomach. This stinky slop is full of lumps and stomach acid.

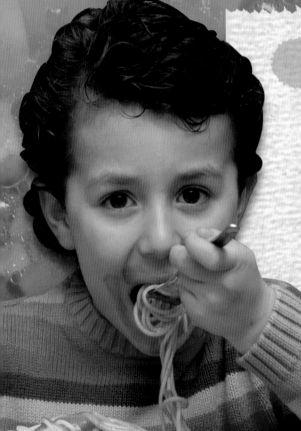

Move along

1. When you swallow, food travels into your stomach.

2. Your stomach makes acids that attack the food and break it down into a lumpy soup called chyme.

3. The chyme moves into a long, loopy coil called the small intestine, which keeps squeezing it along.

4. The walls of the small intestine absorb nutrients that your body needs to stay healthy.

5. What's left goes into another coil called the large intestine, where liquid is absorbed into your body.

But what happens next? Check out the next page for the end of the stomach story!

Time for Number 2s

Meet your bacteria. Lots of them live in your large intestine and they're hungry for the food leftovers that arrive there. These leftovers are things you can't digest, such as tough fiber or some types of sugar. The bacteria munch on it and break it down. Eventually, what remains goes through a tube called the rectum and comes out of your bottom as poop.

Poop. Can it be true?

Do you know poop? Take our true or false quiz on number 2s.

❖ **Poop is brown because you ate brown things.**
FALSE! Along with a whole load of bacteria, water, and leftover food parts, poop contains used-up body cells that are either orange-brown or yellowish. Mixed together, it all makes your poop-color.

❖ **Corn comes out of your body looking exactly the same as when it went in.**
TRUE! (If you don't chew it.) The outer husk of corn kernels is made of material too tough for your body to digest, so if you don't chew them, they travel all the way through you and get mixed into your poop.

❖ **Poop smell is caused by two ingredients called poop-juice and phew gas.**
FALSE! It's caused by two smelly chemicals called skatole and indole. We humans hate the smell of these, which helpfully puts us off eating our own poop (which is lucky, because it would make us very sick).

Your crowd

You've got many millions of bacteria living on you and inside you. Most of these tiny, one-celled living beings are harmless and helpful. You provide a home for them, and in return they help you out.

WAS THAT YOU?

Everybody farts! People do it 14 times a day, on average, so why not count yours up one day to see how well you do on the worldwide fart scale? Here's why you let loose so much.

It wasn't me. It was my bacteria.

Parts of the food you eat are useless to your body, so those go into your large intestine (see page 66). More than 200 kinds of bacteria live there, munching away at these leftovers to break them down. While they're doing that they make smelly gases. How smelly the gases are depends on what you ate. For instance, cabbage has a chemical called sulfur in it, which makes a really stinky fart.

Farting is also caused by swallowing too much air as you eat. The air travels through you and out the other end, or gets pushed back up as a burp.

Alright! So who was it?

Parp!

Fart noises are pretty complicated. The noise depends on how fast your body pushes out the gas and even how fat your buttocks are.

Food fartometer

Some foods make you fart more, because they contain more of the ingredients your body can't use. Carbonated drinks contain types of sugar that give your intestinal bacteria plenty to munch on. And it's generally agreed that **Jerusalem artichokes** (below) are among the worst fart-making foods. Avoid unless you want to win a gas award!

The good manners guide to worrying gas

Farting can cause embarrassment in public, so here are some tips for coping if you let one go accidentally:

❖ The official word for a fart is a flatus (pronounced flay-tus), so to be polite you could say: "Oh sorry. I emitted a flatus."

❖ If you feel uncomfortably gassy, exercise will help move it on through. Going for a walk would be best, in a wide open space away from others.

❖ If you are embarrassed to use the word "fart," there are many other words used to describe it. The good-mannered phrase would be "passing gas." Bad-mannered phrases include "bum belching" or "letting one rip."

❖ If there's a dog around, blame it when you fart. It can't answer back, and doesn't care about farting in public anyway.

What happens if a king burps?

He gets a royal pardon.

THE PEE PAGE

Whether you call it "urine," a "number 1," or a "tinkle," everybody has to go for a pee sometime.

Pee recipe

Urine is 95 percent water and 5 percent used-up body cells, unwanted material from your food, and salt. It's clean when it comes out and only gets smelly when it sits around and bacteria find it.

Kidney action

You have two **kidneys** inside you, shaped like big kidney beans (the beans are named after them). They work really hard for you, washing your blood and making pee. Here's what your kidneys do all day:

1. They wash blood to filter out waste chemicals that your body has made while working. They also wash out any unwanted stuff from the food you ate that had soaked through your stomach wall into your blood.

2. They make sure there is enough water in your body, and get rid of the rest as pee.

3. They send the pee down into a stretchy balloon-shaped organ called a bladder.

4. When your bladder is about halfway full it starts to press on some nerve endings in your body, and you get an "I need to pee" feeling. The pee travels down a tube and comes out when you're ready.

What do you call a dinosaur who always needs to pee?

Toiletosaurus rex

Number 1 facts

❖ When it first comes out, pee is cleaner than spit.

❖ On average, people pee between four and eight times a day.

❖ If you eat asparagus, it will make your pee smell strongly (of asparagus). Asparagus contains a chemical that passes straight through you into your pee.

❖ People used to think pee was yellow because it contained **gold**. They tried all kinds of **experiments** to get gold from it. In fact, a chemical called urochrome makes it yellow.

Champion peeing

You can pee hard or softly by controlling the muscles underneath your bladder. They hold your pee in until you want to go.

Some people drink their own pee because they think it makes them healthier.

71

BACTERIA TO BLAME

Pus-filled zits and smelly sweat can all be blamed on the tiny bacteria that live on your skin.

We love sweat

The biggest crowds of skin bacteria you have live where you make the most sweat, such as under your armpits and on your feet.

A zit's life
This is the story of a little zit that grew and grew, helped by its bacteria friends.

I'm angry now!

1. The zit is born.
Everyone makes skin oil, called sebum. It helps keep your skin soft and waterproof, but sometimes it can block up the little holes in your skin. When it blocks up a hole, it mixes up with dead skin cells. Bacteria love this gooey mess, so they rush over to eat it.

2. The zit grows bigger.
The sebum changes into something called "fatty acid." More and more bacteria crowd around, feasting.

3. The zit turns white.
The body sends in white blood cells to gobble up the bacteria. Then the cells die and turn into creamy-colored pus.

4. The zit dies...
Eventually, the zit will go away if it is treated with an acne cream, which washes away the oil and kills off the bacteria.

5. ...or the zit lives!
The story ending is up to you! If you squeeze a zit, you may spread the bacteria and make it worse. Treat it with acne cream!

Stinky sweat

Stinky armpits or feet are caused by sweat mixed up with hungry bacteria. Your skin makes sweat to help keep you cool. Sweat is a mixture of water, salt, and minerals, and it evaporates into the air (floats away, like steam does from a kettle), taking body heat with it. If it stays on your skin for a while, bacteria start to eat it, creating stinky chemicals while they're snacking. Washing regularly will solve the problem.

Dogs hardly sweat at all, and have to hang out their tongues to get rid of body heat.

CALLING ALL BACTERIA!

❖ The human skin is like a lovely landscape of mountains and valleys. It's a wonderful place for bacteria to live!

❖ The damp, dark, sweaty parts of the human body are best for bacteria.

❖ Don't worry if your human has a wash. Although the sweat and dirt supply will disappear for a while, it'll soon return.

COME TO HUMANLAND
The place where you can eat all day!

⚠ Avoid armpits belonging to humans who use deodorants, which kill bacteria!

73

What you need →

For the severed finger trick
- Some fake blood
- A smallish box with a lid that opens upward*
- Scissors
- Absorbent cotton

For fake blood
- Chocolate ice cream sauce
- Strawberry ice cream sauce
- A few drops of red food coloring
- Bowl and spoon

MAKE YOUR OWN BLOOD

Here's how to make someone think that you found a gruesome severed finger, and make some fake blood that is ideal for Halloween costumes, or just to freak out your friends. The fake blood is edible, so it's ideal for hungry vampires!

SEVERED FINGER TRICK

*If you can't find the right type of box, use an old bandage box. Tape the two ends of the box closed, then cut around three sides to make a flap that opens up like the picture in step 1.

1 Cut a finger-size hole in one side of the box.

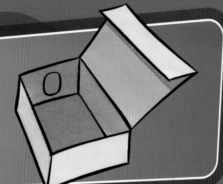

2 Lay some absorbent cotton inside and dab some fake blood on it.

3 Put your finger through the hole and dab fake blood on it.

4 Put the box on the edge of a table, and offer to show someone the severed finger you found. Sit close to the back of the box so that they don't see that you have your finger through the hole.

MAKE FAKE BLOOD

* Mix up a couple of spoonfuls of chocolate and strawberry sauce to get a dark red color. Add drops of food coloring to make it really look like blood.

* If you put this blood on clothes, make sure they're old ones that nobody will mind you messing up. The mixture could stain some materials.

Smell Those Socks!

Do you know someone whose feet are so stinky everybody runs away when they take their shoes off?

Anyone there?

Yep, a few million of us!

Why socks turn crunchy

Socks smell stinky when they soak up sweat and bacteria. When the sweat dries on the material, it turns **stiff and crusty**.

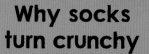

Foot feast

Your feet are lovely sweaty places for bacteria to live because there are thousands of sweat glands in your skin down there (and as you grow up they pump out more and more sweat). Most of the bacteria on your feet are a type called brevibacteria. They like to snack on dead skin cells, and, while they're doing it, they make a chemical called methanethiol. It mixes with your sweat and gives off that well-known cheesy foot smell.

Filthy facts

❖ There are about 250,000 sweat glands on each one of your feet.

❖ Skin bacteria aren't bad. If they didn't eat the dead skin cells you don't need, you'd probably end up with incredibly thick, lumpy, scaly skin.

❖ On average, men have the smelliest feet, because their feet are usually bigger and they sweat more than kids or women.

❖ Nylon socks make your feet smell more, because they trap foot sweat inside them. Cotton socks are best, because they let the sweat through and it evaporates into the air.

The main type of bacteria we have on our feet, brevibacteria, are also used to make some types of smelly cheeses.

Toe cheese

Your feet shed dead skin cells all day long, and they sweat all day, too. The cells and sweat mix into a nice smelly goo, along with tiny parts that rub off your socks and dirt picked up from here and there. Your toes roll the mixture around to make crumbly **toe cheese**, also known as toe jam! A similar smelly mixture collects in the folds of your belly button. See if you can fish some out.

Toe Cheese Man

- 2 cups whole milk
- 4 teaspoons lemon juice or distilled white vinegar
- Saucepan
- Wooden spoon
- Measuring pitcher
- Colander
- Plate
- An adult to help you with step 1 because it's hot

Next time you have a yucky Halloween party, create Toe Cheese Man and tell your friends you made him from the gunk between your toes. Then eat him in front of them! He tastes yummy!

1 Put the milk in the pan and get an adult to help you to heat it up gently on a stove.

The milk will separate into clear liquid and white lumps.

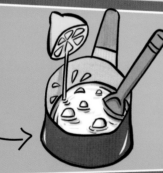

2 When the milk starts to simmer (bubble very gently), stir in the lemon juice or vinegar.

3 Let the mixture stand to cool. Then strain out the white lumps.

4 Squash the white lumps together until they stick in one lump. Then use it to model a man on a plate. Or, instead of making a man, you can give each of your friends a small lump of "toe cheese" and dare them to eat it.

FOOT HORRORS!

Some of the things that can happen to feet sound like they came out of a horror movie!

Attack of the creeping foot fungus!

Athlete's foot is a kind of mold that grows on foot skin and makes it really itchy

Invasion of the cauliflower lumps!

Plantar warts (also called verrucas) make a cauliflower-shape blotch on the skin, speckled with black. They are infectious.

Spread of the cheese-crust bulge!

Lumps of yellowy hard skin called calluses are caused by the way people walk and the position of their shoes.

Trench attack!

Trench foot (also called chilblains) is a burning sensation caused by a foot being cold and damp for too long.

You're So Flaky!

Wherever you go, you sprinkle dead skin cells and dead hairs all over the place. Don't panic, though. You're not falling apart. It's just your skin doing its thing.

Hairy you
You've got hair all over your skin except on the palms of your hands, the soles of your feet, and your lips.

Skin cake

Your skin has got **layers like a cake**. It keeps your insides protected, warms you up, cools you down, and it's even stretchy so it can grow with you.

1. The top layer, made of skin cells, is called the **epidermis**. As the top cells die and fall off, they are replaced by the ones beneath.

2. There are hairs growing out of tubes in your skin, called **follicles**.

3. The layer below is called the **dermis**. It has all kinds of useful things, such as nerve endings (to help you feel), blood cells, and clumps of cells called glands that make oil and sweat.

4. Underneath is a layer of **fat**, which helps keep you warm.

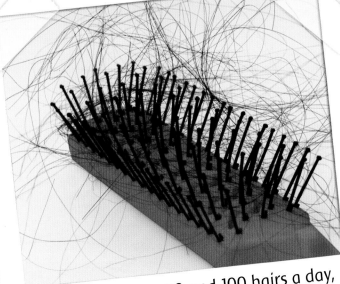

You lose between 50 and 100 hairs a day, but mostly they are replaced by new ones.

Makin' flakes

Your dead skin cells—the ones on top of the epidermis—constantly fall off at a rate of between 30,000 and 40,000 a minute! One person loses roughly 9 pounds of it each year. The tiny flakes usually float away harmlessly, but on some people's heads they get trapped by hairs, then glued into clumps by skin oil. The result is **dandruff**. You start to get dandruff if your scalp (the skin on your head) starts to make too many skin cells or too much oil.

Drop-off zone

All kinds of things can drop off your skin. Don't worry, though. You've got plenty more where they came from.

❖ **Wart away**: A wart is a knobbly clump of skin cells that grows when a type of germ called a virus gets into the skin. Eventually, warts drop off.

❖ **Scabby skin**: If you cut your skin, your blood gathers up a clump of cells, called a clot, to plug the hole. This dries out and becomes a scab that protects the hole while it mends. Then the scab drops off.

❖ **Big blister**: If your skin is rubbed, say, by some tight shoes, it makes a little fluid-filled cushion called a blister to protect itself. Eventually, the blister pops, dries up, and drops off (probably into your socks).

Body Goo to Go

Lucky you! There are a few gooey parts still to discover on yourself.

All about earwax

Next time you see someone wiggle their finger in their ear, watch how they take a secret glance at their finger to see some of their **sticky earwax**. Your earwax is made by thousands of little glands in a tube inside the entrance to your ear, where there are also lots of tiny hairs. The wax and the hairs trap things, such as dust and insects, before they get into your ear's inner working parts. Earwax is made from sweat, body oil, and dead skin flakes.

Eye goo

Why is there yellow crusty goo in the corners of your eyes when you wake up? It's only **dried tears**, and that doesn't mean you've been sobbing in your sleep. Your eyes make tear liquid all the time to wash away dirt and stop your eyeballs from drying out. It contains bacteria-cleaning chemicals plus water, oil, and some mucus (yes, snot) to help it stick to your eye. When you're awake you blink it away, but when you're asleep some of it seeps out and dries on your skin.

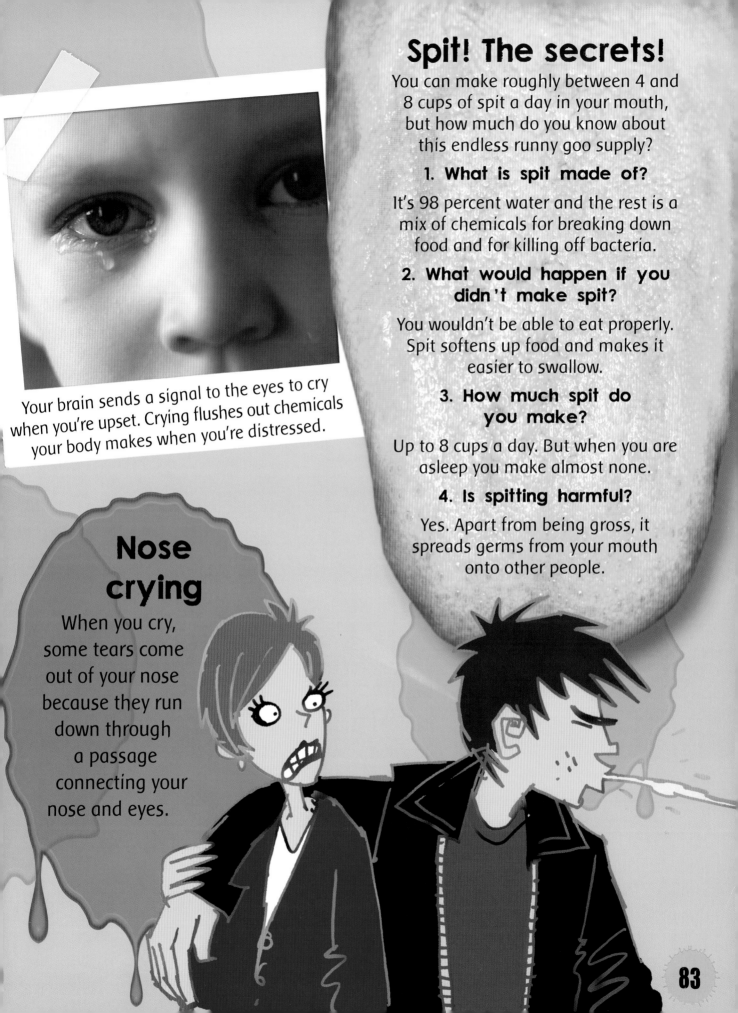

Your brain sends a signal to the eyes to cry when you're upset. Crying flushes out chemicals your body makes when you're distressed.

Spit! The secrets!

You can make roughly between 4 and 8 cups of spit a day in your mouth, but how much do you know about this endless runny goo supply?

1. What is spit made of?

It's 98 percent water and the rest is a mix of chemicals for breaking down food and for killing off bacteria.

2. What would happen if you didn't make spit?

You wouldn't be able to eat properly. Spit softens up food and makes it easier to swallow.

3. How much spit do you make?

Up to 8 cups a day. But when you are asleep you make almost none.

4. Is spitting harmful?

Yes. Apart from being gross, it spreads germs from your mouth onto other people.

Nose crying

When you cry, some tears come out of your nose because they run down through a passage connecting your nose and eyes.

BACTERIA BADDIES

If bad bacteria come along from outside and get into your body, you can end up feeling really sick.

Wash your hands, or weep

Bacteria from your food comes out in your poop (see page 67), and lots of the teeny-tiny critters hang around toilets. Unless you wash your hands after you've been to the toilet, the bacteria stick on your hands and go back into your stomach when you touch your mouth, making you unwell. If you touch things, such as doorknobs, with your unwashed hands, you'll start to **spread harmful bacteria**.

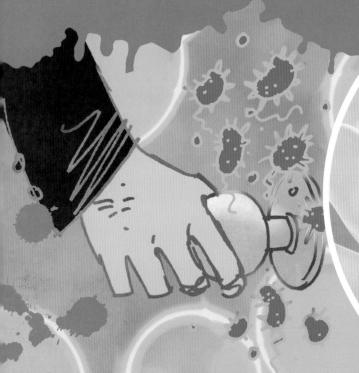

Filthy facts

❖ Restaurant workers who don't wash their hands properly can spread bad bacteria from their toilet to the diners eating the food they cook.

❖ Food left lying around gets more and more bacteria on it, especially if people touch it and pass on bacteria from their hands. Salad bars are the worst for collecting bad bacteria from hands, especially lettuce.

❖ If you bite your nails or suck your fingers, loads of bacteria slip from your hands into your mouth, and you run the risk of swallowing harmful ones.

Keep it hot

Cold water hardly washes off any bacteria from your hands, so always wash them in warm water plus soap.

Your body can usually fight off bad bacteria, but may sometimes need a little help from antibiotic medicine, which kills them.

Yuck! Soap!

And hot water, too. We're doomed!

Badly cooked = bad bacteria

Any food that's not cooked or stored properly can take a whole load of bad bacteria down into you when you swallow it. **Chicken** is particularly dangerous, because the birds have a bacteria inside them called **salmonella** that is harmful to humans. Your body will try to get rid of bad bacteria as quickly as it can by making you vomit and giving you diarrhea.

FREAKY FARM

Farm animals might look peaceful and harmless, but they're hiding some disgusting secrets. No wonder they don't talk!

Cow power

Methane from cow manure is sometimes used to create electricity. Cow poop is even used to make plastics and antifreeze, which prevents icing in engines.

Animal gangs

Farm animals, such as sheep and cattle, live in herds and behave like an animal gang. A cow herd has a leader and some other top cows that boss the rest of the herd around and get to eat and drink first. When the herd moves, the top cows always go at the front. The **gang leaders** sometimes **bully** other cattle by headbutting or pushing them, and though cows in a herd lick each other a lot, as a sign of togetherness, the top cows will lick only each other. They won't bother with the rest.

There are 80 different sheep diseases, including nasal bots, blue tongue, lamb fungus, sheep measles, watery mouth, and pizzle rot.

Champion gassers

Cows have big burping and farting habits. That's because they have a four-chambered stomach armed with bacteria that help them to break down the plants they eat. The food goes into the first chamber for some digesting, then comes back into the cow's mouth for more chewing. After that it travels on through various chambers, while the cow's stomach bacteria are using the food to make stinky gases.

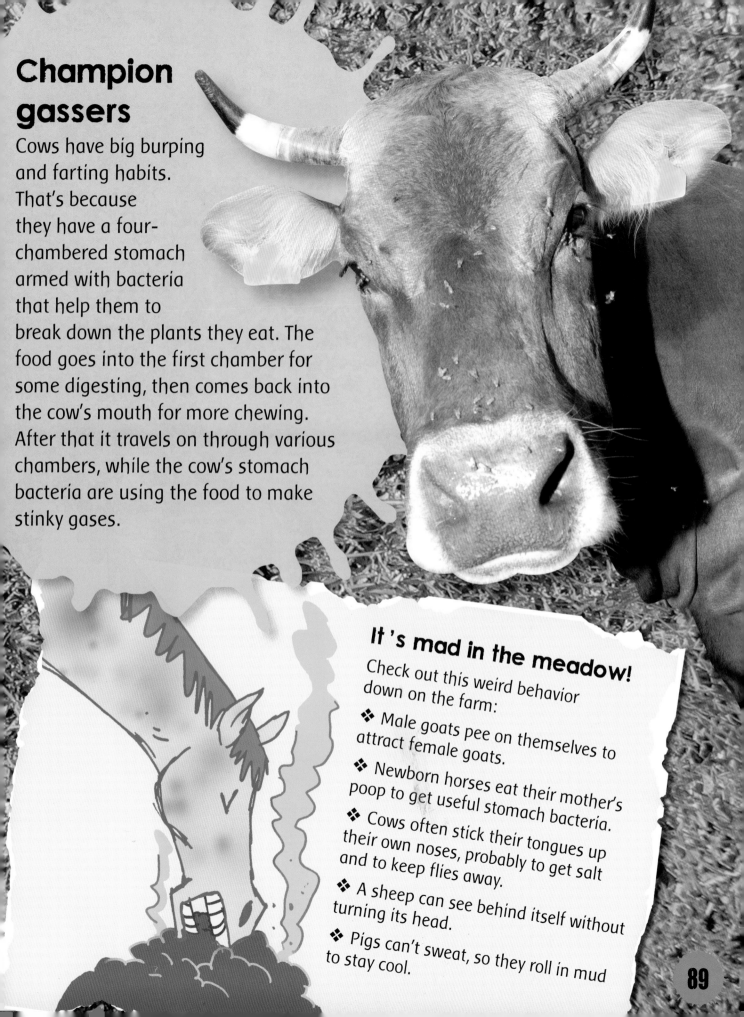

It's mad in the meadow!

Check out this weird behavior down on the farm:

❖ Male goats pee on themselves to attract female goats.

❖ Newborn horses eat their mother's poop to get useful stomach bacteria.

❖ Cows often stick their tongues up their own noses, probably to get salt and to keep flies away.

❖ A sheep can see behind itself without turning its head.

❖ Pigs can't sweat, so they roll in mud to stay cool.

89

PETS—THE YUCKY TRUTH!

Who would have thought our pet friends were so foul? Never mind. We love them anyway...

Here is a breed of dog called a shi poo, a cross between a shi tzu and a poodle. Cute dog, terrible name!

Jump up

Fleas can jump around 200 times their own body length. They're among the best jumpers in the world.

How to be a cat (or dog) flea

1. Mommy flea jumps onto Tiddles, the cat. She sucks Tiddles' blood and lays eggs on his skin.
2. The eggs drop off onto the carpet, where tiny creatures called larvae hatch out.
3. The larvae hide inside protective coats called cocoons, where they slowly turn into fleas.
4. Rover, the dog, comes visiting.
5. The fleas in their cocoons sense Rover's body warmth and the vibration that Rover makes as he walks over the carpet. Yum, yum! He'd make a great home!

Number 2s

Just like us, pets are crawling with bacteria, and some of these are harmful to humans. Nasty bacteria lurk in **pet poop**, and that's why its important for dog and cat owners to scoop up their pet's droppings and dispose of them safely. Always wash your hands if you touch pet poop.

Jump to it boys! There's a dog over here.

DOGS vs. CATS

★★★★★★★★★★★★

IN A GROSS CONTEST, WHO WOULD WIN— POOCHES OR PURRERS? YOU DECIDE.

DOGS...

…have a wet nose all the time. The wetness is mucus (runny snot). It helps the dog to smell, by trapping smell molecules that float past in the air.

…like to smell people, which can be pretty embarrassing. They can even smell human fingerprints.

…like to lick their owners as a sign of friendship. Their spit is pretty clean, but it can smell of the food they have eaten.

…love to roll in the poop of other animals. They like to spread the smell all over themselves.

CATS...

…vomit fur balls when they've licked up too much cat hair.

…make themselves throw up by eating grass.

…sometimes leave piles of poop around their yard, to put off other cats from coming into their territory.

…like to drink the dirty water in puddles.

° 1 teaspoon vegetable oil
° 1 tablespoon salt
° 2 tablespoons all-purpose flour
° 3 tablespoons water
° Bowl and spoon
° Greased baking sheet and oven mitts
° Brown paint and brush
° White craft glue (optional)
° A friendly adult to help you with the oven stage

MIND THE DOGGIE DO!

This pile of fake pet poop is very lifelike, and anyone who sees it will be fooled into thinking that a dog has done a dirty pile where it shouldn't.

1 Make the dough by mixing the oil, salt, and flour together. Add the water gradually to make a mixture that's not too runny.

Roll the dough into a hotdog shape and then wind it into a doggie-poop-shape coil. **2**

3 Put the poop on the sheet and dry it on a very low heat (350 °F). It should take 2–3 hours.* Ask an adult to help you with this hot stage.

*Don't forget the poop is in the oven! Check on it every now and then to see how dry and hard it's gotten. And DON'T try using a microwave.

4 When the poop is dry and cooled down, paint it brown. To make it last longer, you can coat it with white craft glue as a kind of varnish.

To carry out this trick, put the poop in a place where people will see it, but won't accidentally step on it and crush it.

Poop to you

Poop is useful! Elephant and kangaroo poop can be made into paper, for instance. In many parts of the world, dried dung cakes are used as fuel.

What could YOU use your fake poop for?

✱ If you want to make your doggie poop into a tasteful pen-holder, stick a pencil down into it at stage 2 to make a pen-shaped hole.

✱ Send your poop wrapped up in pretty paper in a box, as a thoughtful present to a friend.

✱ Make some mini poops that could become lovely refrigerator magnets for your favorite relatives at Christmas. Remember that mini ones won't need so much cooking.

✱ Hang it on the bathroom door. Your mom will be really pleased!

HORRIBLE HUNTERS

Everybody has to eat, but wild animals don't get given platefuls of grub like we do. If they eat meat, they have to hunt and kill it for themselves. Here are some of the yuckiest hunters around.

Have you ever seen a dried empty insect body on a spiderweb? The **spider** has injected its victim with digestive juices to make its insides liquid, then sucked them out like a milkshake.

The lizard with bad breath

Komodo dragons (below) are the biggest lizards on the planet. They live on a few islands in Indonesia. They grow up to 10 feet long, and they are fierce hunters. Their horrible spit is full of really bad bacteria and, if a victim survives an initial bite from a dragon, it's in for a slow and painful death. The bacteria infect the bite and spread around the body, until the victim dies of blood poisoning. This can take some days. The Komodo hangs around waiting for an easy dinner.

I really, really wouldn't advise coming too close.

Gang warfare

Pack animals often hunt in teams, picking on weak or baby animals. Lions, wolves, and killer whales all work in groups to kill a victim.

Sick sucker

If you ever visit an Atlantic seashore, look for a murder scene! The culprit is a type of sea snail called a **dog whelk**. It hunts mussels and other dog whelks, attaching itself to its victim's shell and slowly boring a hole through the shell to get to the soft body inside. Then it injects chemicals called digestive juices into its helpless victim to turn it to liquid. Finally, it sucks up the slimy mess. The murder evidence is a tiny round hole bored into an empty shell.

WANTED!

HORRIBLE HUNTERS WITH BAD HABITS!

These animal hunters have really gross ways of getting their grub.

Praying mantis—Found in tropical parts of the world. Impales prey, such as caterpillars, on its spiky legs, before tucking in.

Ghost slug—Found in parts of Europe. Sucks up worms like spaghetti.

Ant—Found worldwide. Slices up its prey using its jaws (called mandibles) like a pair of scissors.

Spitting spider—Found worldwide. Spits a mixture of poison and glue at victims from up to half an inch away. This stops prey from escaping so the spider can enjoy a leisurely meal.

Starfish—Surrounds a living victim with its stomach, and starts digesting.

PEOPLE EATERS

The animals on this page have disgusting table manners. Their worst habit is eating humans!

Don't be dinner!
Tips to avoid being eaten.

1. Don't be stupid enough to go anywhere near a hungry human eater. Never ignore warnings.

2. Run faster than a crocodile. Crocs can outrun humans for 30 feet, but then they have to stop for a rest.

3. Lions and polar bears hate shouting.

In Florida, there are more and more homes, and fewer wild places for alligators—so alligators sometimes wander into houses and yards.

Bear banquet

Bears don't mind picnicking on the occasional person. The most vicious ones are polar bears, followed by grizzlies and black bears.

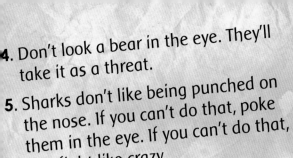

4. Don't look a bear in the eye. They'll take it as a threat.

5. Sharks don't like being punched on the nose. If you can't do that, poke them in the eye. If you can't do that, just fight like crazy.

6. Wear a mask on the back of your head to confuse a tiger. Tigers almost always attack from behind. In India, workers have worn masks on the backs of their heads with good results.

Shark snack

Apparently, sharks don't really like to eat humans. They bite them either accidentally, thinking they are seals, or just out of curiosity to see what they are. Unfortunately, a shark's nibble is pretty deadly, especially if it's a big shark, such as a bull shark or a great white. Sharks hunt by detecting the electrical impulses that muscles make as you move.

Croc criminals

Crocodiles and alligators will both chomp on a human if they're hungry. They like to hide underwater and explode out like a missile to grab prey. Sometimes they spin their prey around and around underwater in a "death roll" to kill it. Crocodiles and alligators prefer to hunt at night, but it's always a bad idea to go swimming anywhere that they usually hang out.

- ½ cup all-purpose flour
- ¼ cup salt
- 2 teaspoons cooking oil
- 3½ tablespoons water
- Leather thong or lace
- Bowl and spoon
- Skewer
- Fork

SHARK'S TOOTH NECKLACE

Remember when you wrestled that shark, escaped, and took one of its teeth to prove it? If nobody believes you, show them your amazing shark's tooth necklace.

1 Mix the ingredients into a smooth salt dough that you can knead.

2 Tear off a piece about the size of a table tennis ball. Mold it into a triangle and shape the tooth by pressing along the top and sides of the triangle with your finger.

3 Use a skewer to make a hole at the top for the lace to thread through.

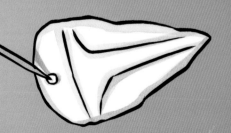

4 Use the prongs of the fork to create the serrated edge of the tooth. Use the points of the fork to make the rough part of the tooth that goes inside the shark's jaw.

5 Cook in a MEDIUM microwave oven for about 60 seconds, until it looks dry and sounds hard when you tap it. If you don't want to cook it, let it to dry for a day or two.

6 Thread the lace through the hole to make a necklace.

Don't bite. Laugh!
Tell these shark jokes next time you wear your tooth necklace. People will "sea" you as a funny person!

Q. What do sharks call humans?

A. Snacks.

Q. Which shark is good at home improvement?

A. The hammerhead.

Q. Which sharks are the best behaved?

A. Angel sharks.

Q. What does a shark eat for dinner?

A. Anything it wants.

Don't Mess with Me!

Animals need defenses to stop their enemies from making a meal of them. These critters take the prizes for the sickest ways to protect themselves.

What smell?

The greatest danger to the skunk is the **great horned owl**, because it likes a skunky snack and it doesn't have a sense of smell.

Stink champion

If a **skunk** gets scared, it **sprays** out **stinky fluid** made in scent glands around its bum. The awful aroma smells like a cross between rotten eggs and burned rubber, with some garlic thrown in. Impressively, the skunk can use its backside muscles to shoot the spray over 20 feet! It will only do it as a last resort, hissing, stamping its feet, and waving its tail first to try to scare off its enemy.

Leaving pieces behind

Lots of lizards drop off their tails to confuse attackers. The tail will keep wriggling for up to 10 minutes to distract the enemy while the lizard escapes. To perform this clever trick, a terrified **lizard** will squeeze strong muscles at the base of its tail to snap the bone inside and **cut the tail off**. The muscles close up the hole to stop blood loss. In a month or so, the lizard will grow a new tail.

Opossums pretend to be dead if in danger. They lie still for up to 4 hours, making a vile smell and leaking green fluid from their bum.

DEFENSE AWARDS

These animals definitely deserve recognition for defending themselves disgustingly.

AWARD FOR EYE-SQUIRTING
Some horned lizards try to confuse an attacker by spouting blood from their eyes. The spray can travel up to 1 foot.

AWARD FOR ARM-GROWING
Some types of starfish can lose limbs and regrow them. A whole new starfish can regrow from just one arm left on a body.

AWARD FOR BEING MESSY
The octopus sends out a cloud of black ink to confuse its enemies. It keeps the ink in a special sac in its body.

AWARD FOR LOOKING SILLY
If it's scared, a porcupine fish can blow itself up to look like a big spiky basketball.

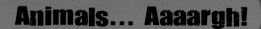

ANIMAL POISONERS

The world's worst poisons come from animals, some of them tiny and peaceful looking. Don't be fooled!

Snake attack

When they bite, **poisonous snakes** pump out venom through tubes in their fangs. How much they inject depends on how angry they are. The land snake with the most lethal poison is the Australian inland taipan, but luckily for us it is very rare and shy. The very worst snake poison comes from a Pacific sea snake, but it's peaceful and won't attack unless it's very scared. Not all snakes are poisonous.

Some snake poison works by shutting down the victim's body and finally stopping the heart.

FILTHY FACTS

❖ Cane river toads are poisonous, and in Australia there are millions of them. They sometimes raid pet food bowls, and occasionally dogs die after licking the toads.

❖ India is the country where snake-bite deaths occur most regularly, with Sri Lanka coming second.

❖ The duck-billed platypus may look cute, but the males have poisonous spurs (spikes) on their heels.

Death by frog

The most poisonous animals on the earth are tiny colorful frogs that live in Central and South America. The poison seeps out of their skin when they are threatened. The **golden poison frog** is the most poisonous, with enough deadly venom in it to kill 10 people. It makes the poison from ants it eats in the jungle, but if it's kept in captivity in a zoo and fed on something else, it stops making the poison and becomes harmless.

The **puffer fish** has a lethal poison in it, and yet people in Japan like to eat it—after cutting out the deadly poisonous parts, of course!

FIDO

103

What you need →

- A plain letter envelope and pe
- A standard-size paper clip
- A thin skinny rubber band
- A metal washer with a good-size hole in it. Ask someone with a toolbox if they have a spare. Find one with a hole that's big enough to put the rubber band through.

RATTLESNAKE EGGS!

Most people know that deadly poisonous rattlesnakes stop their enemies from coming too close by rattling their scaly tails. This little trick copies the noise, and it will make nosy people jump when they look inside the envelope marked "rattlesnake eggs!"

1 Write a warning on the front of your envelope: *WARNING! Contains rattlesnake eggs. Store at a cool temperature, or eggs may hatch.*

2 Unbend the paper clip, and reshape it into a C, with each end bent outward.

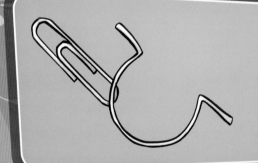

3 Make the rubber band into a figure 8, and double it up. Slip the washer in the middle.

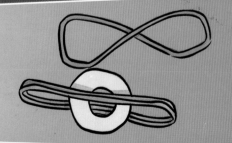

1 **2**

4 Push one half of the rubber band through the washer hole, one way. Then push the other half through the hole, the other way. Pull tight so that the washer sits in the center.

5 Hook the rubber band ends over the ends of the paper clip, and bend the paper clip ends down.

6 Wind the washer around and around for a while. Then slip your trick into the envelope and press it down firmly with your hand.

BABIES GONE BAD

It's not all sweet and cuddly in the animal nursery. Check out the shocking behavior of these animal families.

The first moving object a duckling sees is what it decides is its mother. A scientist proved this by convincing a group of ducklings that a white ball was their mother.

Don't mess with me, dude!

Baby murderer

Some species of cuckoo lay their eggs in other birds' nests, so the babysitting bird gets all the hard work of hatching and feeding the baby. When the chosen babysitting bird is away from her nest, the cuckoo slips in and lays its own egg. When the babysitting bird returns, she is unlikely to notice the extra one. The **cuckoo baby** will hatch before the other eggs and take all the food that the mother brings. Worse still, it will throw the other eggs—and even little newborns—out of the nest.

Filthy facts

❖ Female spiders sometimes eat their male mates. Papa Pie, anyone?

❖ The gray nurse shark gives birth to live babies, called pups. While they are still inside the mother, the babies hatch from eggs and start to grow. But the first ones to hatch eat their brothers and sisters while they're all still inside mom! Eventually, only a couple of babies are born—the strongest surviving baby cannibals.

❖ Adult polar bears, chimps, pigs, hamsters, and wolf spiders have all been known to **eat their own babies**. So next time Mom looks hungry…run!

When **tadpoles** hatch, they will eat any nearby tadpole eggs they find. Sometimes they will even eat other tadpoles.

Mouth nursery

Some fish look after their babies in their mouth. In some species, the mother fish looks after the babies; in other species, it's the father. Sounds like a great idea—unless the fish gets hiccups and swallows!

If a bird realizes it's been tricked and gets rid of a cuckoo egg from its nest, the bullying cuckoo who laid the egg will come and destroy the nest altogether.

ALONG FOR THE RIDE

Some animals have a gruesome way of living off others. These unwanted guests are called parasites. Prepare to be repelled by their gross behavior!

Big wriggler

The largest **parasitic worm** ever found was a jaw-dropping 28 feet long. It came from a sperm whale.

The worm files

Humans are good feeding grounds for parasites. Here's a roll call of nasty ones that people sometimes catch.

Tapeworm: A type of worm with hooks on its head and a flat body. It grabs onto the wall of the intestine and absorbs yummy goodness from the food going by.

Hookworm: A type of worm that lurks in the intestine and sucks blood.

Pinworm: These tiny white worms set up home inside the entrance to your bum, and come out at night to lay eggs. They survive by eating food material from the large intestine (see page 66). You can tell when you have pinworms because they make your bum very itchy.

Brain-jacker

The thorny-headed worm can take over the brain of a pond snail! Its ultimate aim, though, is to get into the body of a **duck**. Here's how this horrible creature works:

1. Worm eggs float in the pond. A pond snail eats a worm egg. It's doomed!

2. The worm hatches in the snail, and makes it create chemicals that affect its brain and change the way it behaves.

3. Instead of doing what it usually does—hiding deep in the pond, away from ducks—the snail goes up the surface and climbs out, making it an easy target.

4. A duck eats the snail, and the worm finds a nice comfy home in the duck's body. The duck and the worm are OK, but the snail is a goner.

5. The duck will poop out the worm's eggs into the pond, and the whole grisly cycle will start again!

Small children are most likely to catch parasitic worms because they play in soil and eat it. The worm eggs get into the soil via animal droppings.

Filthy facts

❖ There can be thousands of parasitic worm eggs in one handful of soil.

❖ A tapeworm can live in a human for up to 20 years.

❖ Flukes are parasitic worms that often live in fish, cattle, and sheep. Humans can become infected by eating undercooked meat and fish or swimming in fluke-infested water.

❖ Almost all living creatures have parasites living on or in them. Most do little harm.

WHOA! THAT'S WEIRD!

Here's a selection of animals who won't be winning beauty contests any time soon.

The **deepsea angler** has its own fishing rod growing out of its head, with a wriggling piece of glowing skin on the end to attract prey.

Down in the deep

Some of the oddest-looking animals live in the deep parts of the ocean. They tend to have no eyes, because it is too dark to see, rows of needle-sharp teeth, and huge mouths to catch as much food as possible. Light-producing organs often help them attract prey. Luckily, they tend to be very small, so they're not going to chomp pieces out of people. Check out photos of gulper eels, viper fish, and hatchet fish.

Screwy-eyed one

Have you noticed something weird-looking about flat fish, such as **plaice**? Their eyes are all askewed! When they are born, they are shaped like ordinary fish, with their eyes on either side of their head. But then, as they grow, one eye moves around and over the fish's head to be with the other one, and the fish ends up looking cross-eyed and squashed.

Bad-beauty contest

Ask your parents or your teacher to help you find images of these creatures on the Internet. Then decide which one gets the "world's silliest-looking creature" award.

- ❖ **Star-nosed mole**—A very stupid-looking critter with a splayed-out nose.
- ❖ **Male proboscis monkey**—Has a nose like a long sausage.
- ❖ **Dumbo octopus**—Big ears and funny arms.
- ❖ **Blobfish**—Like a wobbly gelatin with a strange face.
- ❖ **Yeti crab**—A crab with hairy-looking arms.
- ❖ **Chinese crested dog**—One ugly pooch with a punk hairdo.
- ❖ **Mexican axolotl (below)**—A smiley amphibian that looks like a giant tadpole.

¡Ay, caramba!

ANT ATTACK!

There are billions of ants in the world, lots more than humans. If they were big enough they'd probably eat us all for breakfast!

One, two, three, lift!

Ants can lift about five times their own body weight, but don't worry about being carried away. It would take millions of ants to lift up a human.

Ant exam

Ants can shoot out a poison called formic acid. The ant with the most painful sting is the South American bullet ant. Being stung by one feels like being shot by a bullet. Young men of the Amazonian Satere-Mawe tribe who want to become warriors have to take a painful bullet ant test. They put on a glove containing hundreds of bullet ants and keep it on for 10 minutes. They have to slip on the glove up to 20 more times before they are judged tough enough to be fighters.

WELCOME TO THE ANT CAFE

In some parts of the world, people eat ants. Here's a menu from the imaginary Ant Cafe. Tuck in, before your meal crawls away!

Starter—Escamoles
Escamoles means "ant eggs" in Mexico, where they are a delicacy.

Main course—Ant curry
In parts of India and Southeast Asia, mashed-up ant paste is used to flavor curry.

Pudding—Honeypot ants
Aboriginal Australians like to eat honeypot ants, which are full of the sweet honeydew nectar they have eaten. When the ants pop in your mouth as you chew, the nectar dribbles out.

Marching murderers

Among the toughest ants are **army ants**, found in Africa and South America. Like most ants, they live in big gangs called colonies. But unlike other ants, the army type don't bother to make permanent nests. Instead they stay on the move, resting in temporary, hanging nests that are made from the worker ants themselves. Army ants move in a long column, swarming over any small creatures in their path and eating them alive.

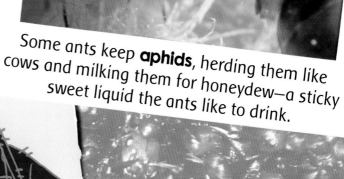

Some ants keep **aphids**, herding them like cows and milking them for honeydew—a sticky sweet liquid the ants like to drink.

What do you call a 100-year-old ant?

An ant-ique.

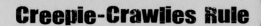

STICKY ICKY SPIDERS

Spiders not only look gross, they act that way, too. Here are some terrible truths about those eight-legged sickos.

LOOK OUT!
SPIDER ABOUT!

Some of the world's most dangerous spiders hang out in places where humans might accidentally meet them.

❖ **Brazilian wandering spider**
Up to 5 inches wide and extremely poisonous, it has been found on bunches of bananas imported from South America.

❖ **Australian funnel-web spider**
Potentially deadly, they lurk in dark spots such as underneath outdoor toilet seats.

❖ **Black widow spider**
The world's fifth most poisonous spider has been found hiding in bunches of grapes imported from California.

Wrapped up ready

Spiders kill their prey by biting them and pumping poison into the bite. To keep the struggling victim quiet as it dies, the spider might wrap it up in a shroud of **sticky thread**. Then the spider might store it for snacking on later. Spiders can only eat liquid, so they pour chemicals into their food to turn it to mush. Luckily most spiders are harmless to humans, but a few have dangerous venom and will bite if they feel threatened.

Boyfriend brunch

Some female spiders eat their mates. The **black widow spider** gets its name because it does this.

Horrible hunters

Spiders have various ways to trap tasty creatures. Some weave sticky web traps. Others carry a little web net to throw over victims. Some **jump out** from hiding places, occasionally leaping up to 80 times their own body length. The jumping spiders are the aggressive, bad-tempered ones and won't run away from humans. Instead they will rear up and display their fangs if a human comes too near.

In Cambodia, people eat fried tarantulas. They taste like chicken, but have a brown goo in the stomach made of eggs, organs, and spider poo!

Apology The author couldn't write any more about spiders because it made her feel all shivery and scared!

- A clean black sock (not one with holes in it, though)
- Old newspaper, paper towels, or clean rags
- Needle and thread
- Four or five fat black pipe cleaner
- Metal washers, or buttons
- Scissors
- White craft glue

SCARY SOCK SPIDER

Make Sam the scary sock spider from an old sock and use him to guard your possessions. Don't worry if he looks more "socky" than "spidery." People who are scared of spiders are usually scared of just about anything with eight legs, and even the word **SPIDER!** so you could just show them this book.

1 Stuff one end of the sock with balled-up paper or rags, to make a fat body. Leave enough room for the head, though.

2 Make a tight knot in the sock to keep the body in place. Then stuff the end to make a head.

3 Sew the end of the sock shut underneath the head.

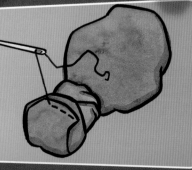

4 Stitch on the pipe cleaners to make four legs on either side. Sew one under the head, and six under the body. Bend the pipecleaners in a couple of places.

5 If your pipe cleaners are long, you can catch the legs up on either side of the body, sewing them so that they stay in place.

6 Use metal washers, or buttons, for the eyes. Stick them on with a dab of PVA glue.

If you like, you can use the fifth pipe cleaner to make fangs. Cut two small pieces and sew them onto the head.

WORMY WONDERLAND

Wriggly earthworms are good for the soil, so we should try to love these slimy little guys.

Pooing goodness

Earthworms eat dead plants and soil. They take out the food they need from them, then poo out the rest in long wiggly tubes called **wormcasts**. The poo is just ground-up soil and plant material, and is harmless to us. In fact, it helps to keep the soil rich and fertile. The beach is a good place to spot wormcasts, made by a similar type of worm called the lugworm. Instead of eating soil, lugworms eat sand and poo it out as small piles on the beach.

Liftoff!

Worms have traveled into space on board the **Space Shuttle**, so astronauts could study how they coped in weightlessness. Luckily they didn't escape and start floating around!

Yummy, lunch!

Know your worm

Earthworm bodies are made of sections called **segments**. If a worm loses its back end, it can grow a new piece, if it has enough segments at the front. If it gets cut in half too near its head, it will die. You can tell when a worm has had an accident and lost its butt because its back end grows back a lighter color.

Filthy facts

Here are some disgusting facts about our slimy, wriggly friends:

❖ **Moles eat earthworms**, squeezing them like a tube of toothpaste first to push their soily poo out.

❖ An earthworm is a hermaphrodite, which means it is both male and female.

❖ Earthworms lay tiny eggs which are wrapped up in a protective cocoon and left in the soil.

❖ You can order earthworm poo and eggs through the mail, to help make a garden more fertile.

❖ The largest species of worms **live in hot countries**. Some types can grow up to 10 feet long.

SLIMEBALLS IN SHELLS

Imagine if you left a trail of gooey snot behind you wherever you went. Snails and slugs do just that. They're like walking runny noses!

Snail medicine

For centuries doctors prescribed snails as medicine. Boiled snail pulp was used on burns and snail mucus was smeared on sore skin.

Goo to go

Snails move by squeezing and then relaxing their muscles, so they ripple along. Despite skimming on a path of slime, they move famously slowly. That gives them plenty of time to look around—their eyes are on the ends of their longest tentacles. Snail goo won't harm you and snails don't bite. They're just annoying to gardeners and farmers because they munch on plants.

Who you calling butthead?

The giant African land snail grows up to 1 foot long and lays an egg more than 2 inches wide. Its snail trail must be pretty sticky!

It's not easy being a snail...

Slimy slugs

Slugs are types of snail without a big shell. They leave slimy trails just like their snail cousins, and constantly make goo to cover their bodies, because if they dry out too much they die. Their trail goo contains tiny fibers to stop the slug from slipping backward if it's climbing up the side of something. There are lots of different types of slugs in various yucky colors, but they all have one weird thing in common. A slug's butt is on the back of its head!

❖ Most slugs eat plants, but some slugs will hunt down and eat other slugs by following their sticky trail.

❖ Some freshwater fish eat water snails by sucking them out of their shells.

❖ Birds will pick up snails and drop them onto the ground to smash their shells, before pecking out the body.

❖ Gardeners put down slug pellets —poison-laced lumps of cereal— that slugs like to snack on.

❖ Gardeners may also spread tiny nematode worms on the garden. The worms slip into slugs through the hole behind their head and infect them with deadly slug-killing bacteria.

War in the Water

Ponds may look like peaceful places, but they're really vicious battlegrounds between creepie-crawlies, each trying to outdo the other with their disgusting behavior.

Little but lethal

Pond water is full of tiny wriggly creatures, many of them too small to see. They all have one thing in common—something's out to kill them, and here's how:

Diving beetles ambush their prey and tear it to pieces.

Water spiders stab their prey with their sharp mouth parts.

Dragonfly babies (called nymphs) shoot out a weird unfolding bottom lip to swallow any passing creatures.

Dragonflies hover and swoop above the pond, grabbing tasty flies and mosquitoes in mid-air between their spiky legs.

Luckily none of these creatures is big enough to eat humans, though dragonfly nymphs might bite us.

Dragonflies have giant eyes. So imagine what it would be like to meet one in prehistoric times when they had wingspans 3 feet wide!

Mmm! I'll have a fly for dinner.

Aargh! It got me!

Filthy facts

Warning: Disgusting nasties may lurk in ponds and rivers.

❖ The Amazon candiru fish is attracted by pee. It will swim up inside a peeing swimmer's body (through the place where they pee) and get stuck. Ouch!

❖ A serious illness called Weil's disease is caught from rat pee mixed into dirty water.

❖ Freshwater crayfish will nip swimmers with their sharp pincers. They look like mini lobsters and are very bad-tempered.

Sick Smoothie

Baby diving beetles are called **water tigers** because they are so fierce. They pierce their enemies and suck out their insides like a sick smoothie.

Mmm. Sweet.

Pick up a sucker

In hot countries, swimmers in lakes and rivers could find themselves with an unwanted passenger stuck on their skin—a slimy **leech** getting fat as it sucks their blood. A leech is a type of worm that can hang on tight, increasing its body size 11 times after a blood dinner. Leeches don't harm humans and doctors sometimes use them in medical care. They can be hard to remove, though.

- Two pieces of 9 in x 12 in construction paper, in strong colors.
- Ruler
- Pencil
- Scissors
- White craft glue
- Marker pens, crayons or paint

Pop-up Critter

This 3D tough-looking insect makes a great pop-up card, or add a tongue to make it into a picture to display.

1 Fold the two pieces of paper in half as shown.

2 Measure halfway down the lighter-colored paper. Cut 2 in in from this point.

3 Fold up the corners of the cut as shown. Run your finger along the folds to make them sharp.

4 Unfold the paper and open it out. Then use your fingers to gently strengthen the folds, to make an open mouth as shown.

5 Spread glue over the back of the "mouth" card, only around the outside of the mouth. Press it down onto the darker piece of paper, matching the fold down the middle so that your card will close flat.

6 Now draw or paint on your insect. Give it weird insect eyes, antennae, six legs, and two more body parts (most insects have three altogether).

If you want to add a tongue, cut a strip of paper and roll it up on a pencil to make it curly Then glue it into your insect's mouth. Remember that if you do this, your picture will not lie flat as a pop-up card.

BUG BABIES

Do you think babies are cute? Perhaps you'll change your mind when you find out about vicious insect babies. They're more likely to make you say "Yuck!" than "Aaah."

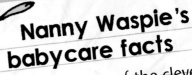

Nice to eat you!

Wolf spiders make good moms, carrying their creepy-crawlie spider babies around on their back.

Nanny Waspie's babycare facts

Here are some of the clever ways insect parents cope with their little treasures:

❖ Mother stink bugs smother their eggs in bacteria. A nice bacteria brunch will be their babies' first yummy meal when they hatch.

❖ Parasite wasps lay their eggs on other insects and when the babies hatch, they munch through their helpless host.

❖ In springtime look for gobbets of frothy spit on plant stalks. It's made by baby froghopper insects, who hatch and then make the foul-tasting froth to protect themselves from enemies.

❖ Burying beetles lay their eggs near a dead animal body they have buried, there will be lots of rotting flesh for t babies to feast on when they hatch.

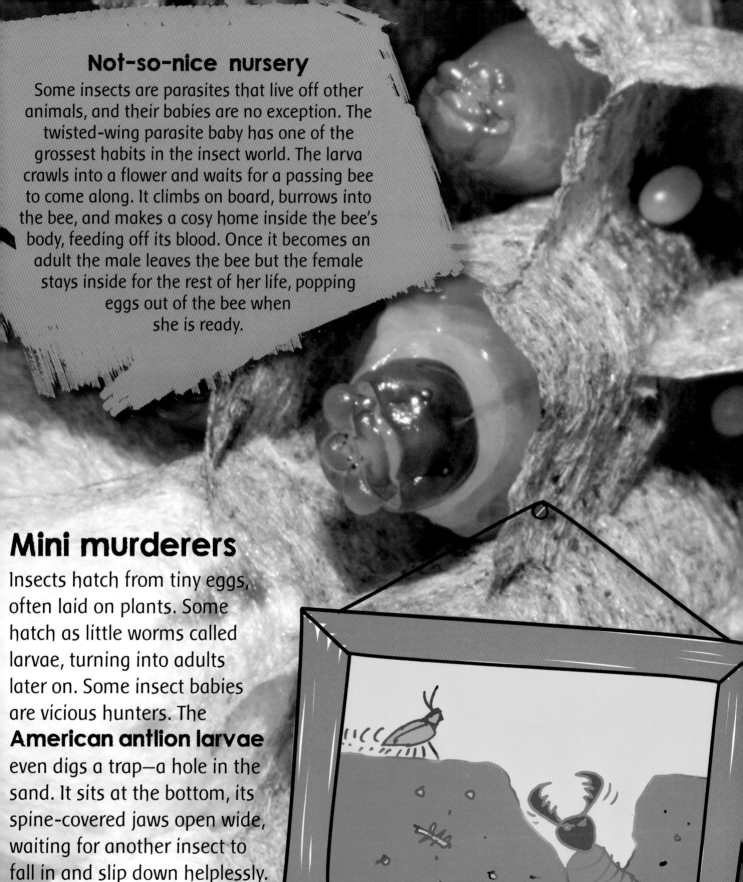

Not-so-nice nursery

Some insects are parasites that live off other animals, and their babies are no exception. The twisted-wing parasite baby has one of the grossest habits in the insect world. The larva crawls into a flower and waits for a passing bee to come along. It climbs on board, burrows into the bee, and makes a cosy home inside the bee's body, feeding off its blood. Once it becomes an adult the male leaves the bee but the female stays inside for the rest of her life, popping eggs out of the bee when she is ready.

Mini murderers

Insects hatch from tiny eggs, often laid on plants. Some hatch as little worms called larvae, turning into adults later on. Some insect babies are vicious hunters. The **American antlion larvae** even digs a trap—a hole in the sand. It sits at the bottom, its spine-covered jaws open wide, waiting for another insect to fall in and slip down helplessly. Then…crunch, gulp! That's one more meal for the antlion and one less insect in the world.

Antlion Baby Photo

FIENDISH FLYERS

Flies are the champions of creepie-crawlie grossness. Not only are they disgusting, they can be deadly, too.

What's the difference between a fly and a mosquito?

A mosquito can fly, but a fly can't mosquito.

Sick on your snack

Keep your food away from houseflies because, if one lands, here's what it will do:

1. Taste the food with its feet, and drop off any germs it might be carrying. It likes to eat poo to get water, so may have just come from eating that.

2. Vomit on the food to make it more runny and easier to suck up.

3. Pee on your plateful—a fly pees every few minutes.

Filthiest flies ever

Here are the yuckiest flies around:

Flesh fly—Likes to eat rotting meat.
Horse fly—Sucks animal blood.
Face fly—Munches on mucus in animals' noses.
Bot fly—Lays its eggs in animals' skin. The fly hatches and emerges out of a lump on the skin.
Blow fly—Likes to tuck into a pile of animal poo.

Big-time bloodsuckers

Female mosquitoes are the world's worst killers of animals and humans. Every year up to a million people die and many more become sick because of serious diseases the females can pass on when they **suck blood**. They pierce the skin and put their spit into the wound to keep the blood flowing while they feed on it. It's the spit that makes a mozzie bite itch so much.

Bad-smelling bloom

Some flowers smell gross to attract flies, which help to pollinate them. The **Dead Horse Arum** is a fly-loving flower. Guess what it smells like…

A maggot is a baby fly. Maggots eat just about anything, including rotting flesh and sewage.

BUZZING BEASTIES

"Buzz, buzz..." Let's hope that's a laid-back little bee or a chilled-out wasp, not a berserk buzzer with its sting pointing your way!

The bad side of bees

OK, bees are generally good. They help to pollinate flowers and make yummy honey. But they have a bad side, especially if they are Africanized killer bees, a type found in the Americas. It's easy to upset them, just by walking near their nest. If they think their home is under threat they will swarm angrily and follow an enemy for a long distance, stinging all they can and continuing to attack for up to 24 hours. Now, that's a bad temper!

Queen killers

Bees will sometimes kill a queen bee in their colony by **"queen balling"** her, squeezing around her in a tight ball until she overheats and dies. This sometimes happens when a beekeeper tries to put a new queen into a beehive.

This is a sticky situation.

A **beewolf** is a type of wasp that attacks and paralyzes bees with its sting, then carries them off to feed its young.

Not so sweet

Bees and wasps buzz around being disgusting, just like the rest of us.

❖ Sweat bees are a type of bee that likes to lap up human sweat, to collect the salt from it.

❖ A lone bee can come under attack from a robber fly when it's out collecting pollen. The fly kills and eats the bee.

❖ Wasps build their nests from chewed-up wood mixed with spit.

Wasps at war

Wasps use their sting to kill spiders, caterpillars, and ants. They will try to raid honeybee hives to steal honey and even baby bees to eat. They also use their sting to defend themselves, and it contains a chemical that acts as a kind of alarm for other nearby wasps to come and help. If you get stung by a wasp near a crowded wasp's nest, you'd better get away fast! The nest might contain hundreds or even thousands of wasps, all ready to defend their home.

How do bees get to school?

On the school buzz.

133

HEAVYWEIGHTS

Luckily, giant insects only turn up in horror movies, right? Wrong!

Creepie-crawlie crowd

Locusts look like big crickets, but it's when they get together in swarms that they qualify for the outsize insect page. Sometimes a swarm can cover hundreds of square miles, with millions of locusts turning the sky dark and making a deafening noise. They eat plants, and a big swarm can eat tens of thousands of tons of plants in a few days, completely destroying farm crops. If they don't get enough plant food, they start eating each other.

Which insect can tell the time?

A clock-loach.

The **goliath beetle** grows over 4 inches long. It won't harm you but it could give you a fright, because when it flies it sounds like a small helicopter.

The giant wetas of New Zealand grows as big as a small bird. It will bite and scratch humans if it gets annoyed.

Horror hornet

The Japanese giant hornet lurks in the countryside of East Asia, and sounds not only disgusting but scary, too. It can grow to about 2 inches long (about the size of an adult human's little finger) and it has a massive ¼-inch sting that carries strong venom which can kill allergic humans. Apparently its **sting** feels like a **hot nail** being driven into the skin. Ouch! This horrible hornet has a hobby of attacking honeybee hives and killing the bees inside by cutting off their heads with its powerful jaws.

Filthy facts

Here are some more facts to frighten your friends with!

❖ In Japan, live beetles can be bought from vending machines, as pets.

❖ To make themselves perform better, Japanese **athletes drink giant hornet juice**, a sports drink based on the stomach juices of giant hornet larvae.

❖ In Nigeria, people eat cooked locusts, which taste like shrimp.

❖ Giant rhino cockroaches are kept as pets by some people. They grow over 3 inches long, and like to be stroked.

MUTANT BUG

Invent your own mutant weirdo bug to take over the world, or just hang it it up outside your bedroom door to freak out your mom. It uses recycled materials, so it may be super-ugly, but it's an eco-friendly critter.

- A pair of latex disposable gloves
- Permanent marker pens or acrylic paint
- Rubber band
- Old but clean plastic bags, or a black garbage bag
- Cardboard egg box
- Scissors
- Three clean clear plastic cups
- String
- Kitchen sponge (optional)

1 Blow up the rubber gloves and tie a knot at each wrist like you would a balloon. Draw on bug eyes with permanent marker or acrylic paint and fix the gloves together with a rubber band.

2 Cut twelve long strips of plastic from the bags. Tie three together at one end and braid them to make the legs. Knot at the other end, too. Make six legs altogether.

3 Cut six cups from the egg box. Pierce a small hole in each box section, and also in the bottom of each plastic cup.

136

4

Tie a knot in the end of a long piece of string and thread it through a plastic cup, then two egg cups facing different ways. Do this until you've used up all the egg cups and plastic cups.

5

Glue a pair of legs into the egg cups as shown.

6

Push the egg cups and the plastic cups together to create a silly bug body. Tie the rubber gloves at the top. Make a loop at each end of the string to hang up your mutant bug. You can make a beak by cutting out two pieces of kitchen sponge and then tying them to the knots on the gloves.

You don't need to stick to our wacky mutant bug design. You could invent your own unique version of a bug using recycled boxes, cardboard tubes, and anything else you can think of! Make it as silly as you can!

Wonderful World

SHOWERS, SNAKES, AND SHRUNKEN HEADS

How would you like to go to a place that's dark, dangerous, and feels like a sauna? Then the rain forest is for you!

The truth about Amazonia

Amazonia is the biggest rain forest, stretching across South America. It's warm and it rains every day there, so it often feels like being in a steamy, slightly smelly bathroom. It's gloomy beneath the tall trees, and unknown creatures screech and howl above. Apart from that, it floods regularly and is home to stinging ants, leeches, huge snakes, flesh-eating piranha fish, giant spiders, and vampire bats. If you can put up with all that, though, it's an incredible place.

AMAZON NASTIES

GOLIATH BIRD-EATING SPIDER—Growing up to 1 foot wide, this South American spider can bite or fire its body hairs at you like tiny spears, making your skin sore.

PIRANHA FISH—There are lots of different Amazonian species of piranha fish. Some have sharp teeth and attack in shoals, ripping flesh off their victims. Amazonian Indians use their teeth as hair combs.

There are real-life, **blood-drinking bats**, like in *Dracula*, living in Amazonia. They live on the blood of mammals, and may pass on the deadly disease of rabies.

The world's largest snake is the Amazonian common anaconda. It grows up to 20 feet long and kills prey by squeezing it to death in its giant coils.

Can I have your head?

Visitors were not always welcome in the rain forests of the world. In the jungles of Borneo and the Amazon, **headhunters** once killed enemies and intruders. They cut off their heads and shrunk them as trophies to put on display. In a special ceremony, the **heads were boiled with herbs** to preserve them, and then hung up as grizzly decoration. The headhunters thought that this would give them their enemy's power and stop evil spirits from attacking.

Seriously... there are a few awful creatures in the rain forests, but they are spectacular places full of all kinds of life. The jungles of the world are disappearing quickly, mostly due to logging. This destroys the homes of the people and animals who live there, affecting the world's climate. Now THAT's disgusting.

Project

- Apples (make two or three heads if you can, carving the face in different ways)
- A vegetable peeler
- A plate
- 1/3 cup lemon juice
- 2 teaspoons salt
- Some wooden toothpicks or thin clean sticks from outdoors (optional)
- Some colored yarn (optional)
- Cloves and raisins (optional)

SHRUNKEN HEAD COLLECTION

You can make your own shrunken head! We don't mean go and steal your enemy's head. All you need is an apple and a couple of weeks' worth of patience. You could time it to be ready to display on Halloween night.

1 Peel the apple, carefully digging out the stalk on the top.

2 Use the peeler to carve a face into the apple. Make it look three-dimensional, with human-shaped eye hollows and a straight gash for the mouth.

3 Carve gashes on either side of the nose, and some cheekbone gashes. These hollows will help to make the head look realistic when it dries.

4 If you want to, you can cut the stick into small pieces and stick it along the mouth and in the eyes. That way your head will look authentically "sewn up."

5 Mix the lemon juice and salt together in a bowl and put your apple in it. Let it soak overnight (this helps to stop it going moldy). Then take it out and let it dry on a plate. Put it somewhere safe, such as a kitchen cabinet or a closet. In a week or two it'll look perfect.

If you want to add hair, gently push some long wisps of yarn into the top of the apple.

To add eyes, gently push cloves or raisins into the eyeholes.

Some shrunken science

Your apple dries up because the water in it evaporates over time. Tiny water molecules float out of the apple and away into the air, until there's very little left.

Desert Delights

What do you mean you forgot the map!!!

If you want to be a desert explorer, be prepared to deal with sandstorms, boiling-hot temperatures, and a few unfriendly critters.

A mirage is a pretty sick trick if you're dying of thirst!

Some desert travelers imagine seeing a shimmering lake, when there is none. It's a trick of the light, called a mirage.

Sandstorm surprise

Winds can whip up desert sand and dust to create giant clouds that race across the ground. A sandstorm coming toward you can look like a towering cliff wall! If you were in its path, you would be scratched by the pelting sand grains whipping into your eyes and nose. If you were lucky enough to have a camel, you could shelter behind it. A **camel** can shut its nose to keep out the sand and has **extra eyelashes** to protect its eyes. Later on, if you ran out of food, you could eat the camel!

Be careful you don't sit on a desert cactus. The dagger-sharp spines are hard to remove.

Hot and cold

Deserts are places where less than 10 inches of rain falls a year. If you went on a desert trip and didn't plan properly, here's what can happen to you:

❖ You can die from dehydration (lack of water). In hot deserts, the water in your body will evaporate (disappear) in a day or two, unless you drink to replace it.

❖ You can freeze to death. Some deserts are very cold, particularly at night.

❖ You can get lost. Some deserts are very large.

❖ You can starve. Very few people live in deserts, and there is definitely no fast food!

SNUG IN YOUR SLEEPING BAG?

Some yucky creatures might like to crawl in with you on your desert camping trip...

❖ Scorpions like dark places, such as sleeping bags and shoes. They have poisonous, stinging tails.

❖ A poisonous, biting lizard, the Gila monster, lives in the Mexican desert. Luckily, it moves very slowly.

❖ Snakes like hot places, such as deserts, and might like to curl up for a cozy sleep somewhere they're not wanted.

145

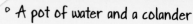

What you need

° A pot of water and a colander
° A friendly adult to help you with the oven stage
° A couple of eggs

For the thousand-year-old egg
° Green and yellow food coloring
° Bubble wrap
° Paper towels
° Kitchen sponge

For the sheep's eye
° Cream cheese
° An olive stuffed with a red pimento, sliced in half
° A small kitchen knife

Faraway Café

Next time you come back from a vacation, serve some food from far away to impress your guests. They'll watch amazed at your bravery as you eat thousand-year-old eggs and sheep's eyes.

For both projects

1 Put the eggs in the pot of water, bring it to a boil, and boil for five minutes.

Thousand-year-old eggs are a Chinese delicacy. The eggs are preserved (traditionally using horse pee), so they come out gloopy and cheesy when they're split open. They're not really a thousand years old. They're usually less than a hundred days old, but that still makes them very old eggs!

2 Take the pot off the heat, pour the contents into the colander, and let the eggs cool down thoroughly. Then shell them and pat them dry with paper towels.

For the thousand-year-old egg

1 Wipe or sponge a very small amount of yellow food coloring into bubble wrap. Roll the egg over it, holding it by the pointed end.

2 Do the same technique with green food coloring. Roll the egg around and around the bubble wrap until you're happy with the effect. Then let the egg dry.

FOR THE SHEEP'S EYE

1 For the sheep's eye, Cut the boiled egg in half and gently pry out the yolk.

Sheep's eyes are a great delicacy in North Africa. They're usually boiled up in a pot along with the rest of the head. Then guests are offered them as treats. To refuse is an insult.

2 Fill the hole with cream cheese and push in the olive half.

147

Chilly Trips

Visiting the far north or south of the world is a dangerous vacation choice, especially because it could involve pieces of you dropping off!

Past polar explorers have had to eat their husky dogs or (it's rumored) each other to survive starvation.

Freezing fingers

The Arctic (in the north) and Antarctica (in the south) are the coldest places on the earth. In wintertime, these snowbound wildernesses are so cold that bare human flesh can freeze within a minute. That's when **frostbite** sets in. First the flesh turns white; then it turns black and blistered. Eventually, it may rot and need cutting off. Fingers, noses, and toes are most at risk.

Anyone got a flashlight?

The North and South poles both have six months of darkness during winter, because of their position in relation to the sun.

I want to go home.

YOU ARE NOT ALONE...

The poles might be empty places, but there are other critters braving the ice—and they're out to get you.

POLAR BEARS—These Arctic bad guys have a great sense of smell. They have claws as sharp as a tiger's, and can run fast. They grow up to 10 feet long, and are partial to humans for dinner.

LEOPARD SEALS—These Antarctic seals have nasty, sharp teeth and are fast swimmers. They attack inflatable boats and will occasionally try to bite divers or people standing on ice near the sea.

ARCTIC LION'S MANE JELLYFISH—This big ball of jiggling jelly has poisonous stinging tentacles that can trail out to an incredible 118 feet.

Antarctic adventure

Antarctica is the coldest and stormiest location on the earth, and nobody lives there permanently, though scientists stay there to study. To keep the environment in good condition, everyone who visits Antarctica must **take home their garbage**, including all their pee and poop. It gets flown or shipped home. (It is impossible to pee outside anyway, because it is too cold—see "Freezing fingers" and work it out for yourself!)

MOUNTAIN MADNESS

Mountains are dangerous places, and surprisingly messy, too. After all, there aren't usually any garbage cans or restrooms, and it turns out that some mountaineers have been pretty disgusting litterbugs…

Top o' the morning to ya

It's now possible to use a **cell phone** on top of Everest. The first ever call was made by a mountaineer in 2007.

In trouble up top

Many people have **died on Everest** and more than 40 bodies have been left to freeze on the mountain's north face, because they are too hard to carry down. Other climbers see them as they pass. High up, air pressure is much less than down at ground level and this causes body changes that can lead to death. It's called altitude sickness. Affected climbers can collapse and die where they stand. Mountaineers have to train hard and take the right gear for their mission, or end up frozen forever.

HE CLIMBED TOO HIGH…

Make me a coffee. I'll be home in two ticks!

FILTHY FACTS

Mountaineers must be crazy! Here's why...

❖ Icy mountains are often zigzagged with crevasses, giant splits in the ice impossible to escape from if you fall in.

❖ If you were unlucky enough to tumble down a crevasse, your body might be trapped in the ice, preserved, and found many years later.

❖ Everest mountaineers aren't just insane, they're often smelly, too, because local guides believe the best way to ward off altitude sickness is to eat lots and lots of stinky garlic soup. Nobody knows if this really helps.

Mountains of garbage

The slopes of the world's most popular mountain climbs are littered with garbage left behind by climbers.
The highest mountain, Everest, is strewn with ropes, oxygen bottles, and even piles of human poop. On Mont Blanc in the European Alps, some of the ice is so polluted by pee that it has turned yellow. Eco-friendly mountaineers do clean-up climbs, when they pick up as much garbage as they can.

Mont Blanc, in the European Alps, even had an old washing machine dumped on its slopes by a litterbug.

MESSY WEATHER

Can weather be disgusting? It can when it drives you nuts, deafens you, poisons you, or rains frozen frogs!

Wind gone wrong

Giant spinning funnels of wind called tornadoes or twisters turn up in the United States and Australia (where they're called willy-willies). They rip up the countryside as they pass through. Sometimes they pick up crowds of animals from below, most commonly groups of frogs or fish. Occasionally, the animals have been taken up so high they freeze and deliver an extra-painful surprise when they fall back to the ground as icy animal lumps!

Why is it so windy at sports events?

Because of all the fans!

Maddening weather

A strong wind called the mistral blows over the south coast of France in November, and is said to **drive people mad**.

Raining again

On the island of Kauai, **Hawaii**, it might be worth opening an umbrella store at the base of Mount Wai'ale'ale. Here it rains for a record-breaking 350 days of the year. The **ground** here is so **muddy** that hardly anyone can visit. Or how about selling waterproof boots at Tutunendo, Colombia, which gets the most rain in the world. A drenching 463 inches of rain fall there on average each year.

Rain may contain dirt, dust, and toxic chemicals made by industrial pollution, too.

FILTHY FACTS

Weather can be stinky... Here's how:

❖ Smog is pollution-filled fog that envelops industrial cities. It can be deadly poisonous as well as smelly.

❖ London, England, was once so polluted by coal smoke that poisonous thick yellow fog, nicknamed a "pea souper," often enveloped the city.

❖ Being "downwind" means being in the path of a wind. If it carries smells, perhaps from a farm, the stink will waft over you.

❖ Deer have such a good sense of smell they can detect your body odor on the breeze if they're standing downwind from you.

WACKY WORLD PARTIES

Around the world there are some pretty strange and weird festivals for fans of disgustingness to visit.

Beat the bull

In July, **bulls are set free** to run through Pamplona in Spain. People run in front to prove their bravery (or stupidity).

Messy-fests

Some festivals need a lot of clearing up afterward. For instance, in March, Indians throw paint at each other during the festival of Holi. The world's **biggest tomato fight** goes on in Spain, in August, during Valencia's Tomato Festival. In Mali, in spring, they have a mud-plastering festival, when everyone slaps mud on the local buildings and on themselves.

You are invited to...

As a fan of "messy stuff," you'll be dying to go to...

❖

The World Bog Snorkeling Championship, held in August in Wales, UK. Snorkel through deep puddles of mud.

❖

The Rattlesnake Round-Up, in Sweetwater, Texas, in March. Take part in the rattlesnake-eating contest.

❖

The Songkran Festival in Thailand in April: basically one big water fight.

❖

Blobfest in Pennsylvania, in July. The crowd reenact scenes from an old sci-fi movie called The Blob, in which jelly aliens invade Earth.

❖

A fishing-throwing contest called **The Interstate Mullet Toss**, in April. Mullet fish are thrown over the state line between Alabama and Florida.

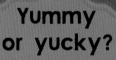

Yummy or yucky?

Food is important at parties, especially at the Thorrablot midwinter feast in Iceland. Because there are only two hours of sunlight a day in Iceland in February, the Icelanders cheer themselves up with a big party and a buffet of seal flippers and rotting shark meat (see page 202). And if you're not a fan of vegetables, avoid Hawaii in November, when there's a Taro Harvest Festival. The taro is a brown-colored vegetable, and at the party you can enter a taro-mush eating contest.

Yeah, what do you want?

In September shark callers gather for the Malangan Festival in Papua New Guinea. They can call sharks, which they then kill and eat.

BEASTLY BEACHES

Beaches are beautiful places... apart from the stinky seaweed and the pollution, that is.

Pollution Cove

Don't go swimming in the sea after heavy rain, because that's when sewage gets washed out of overflowing drains and flows into the sea. If you see a beach with cotton swabs on it, don't swim. Cotton swabs are flushed down the toilet by people, and they are a sure sign that raw untreated sewage has flowed into the nearby water.

Why do beaches smell?

People used to think that going to the seashore was a very healthy thing to do because of the smell of "ozone," which was meant to be good for the lungs. In fact, the reason the seashore smells is not because of ozone but because of rotting seaweed trapped below the sand or in among the rocks. It's not harmful but it is stinky and slimy.

I really hope that was seaweed I stood on!

Shellfish, such as mussels and winkles, filter out material, including raw sewage, from the water and eat it.

Why does the ocean roar?

Because it has crabs on its bottom!

It's not sewage...

Creamy-colored sea scum washed up on a beach is caused by harmless little organisms called algae that live in the seawater.

Shoved on the shore

The Ocean Conservancy organization arranges **beach cleanups** around the world. On a 2007 one-day cleanup of beaches in 76 countries, nearly 3,000 tons of garbage was picked up by volunteers. In 2007, the beach cleaners found, among other things:

❖ 237 ocean animals trapped in garbage
❖ 2 million cigarette butts
❖ 1.2 million bottles and cans
❖ 580,000 bags
❖ 325,000 drinking straws
❖ 61,000 balloons
❖ 30,000 fishing nets

Sick Cities

Nowhere is there more yucky garbage, sewage, and traffic pollution than in the world's big cities.

Trash above

All the trash that's left lying around in big cities is a big problem. The Indian city of Mumbai has an unusual way of getting rid of the awful smell of its 300-acre garbage dump. It pours thousands of gallons of **deodorant** on it!

Critters below

Sewage tunnels and pipes stretch for miles across cities, and they're a great place for rats and mice to live. Nobody knows exactly how many rats there are in any one city, but it's safe to say there is likely to be a big crowd! Wild rats can carry diseases, which they pass on in their droppings, so they're not a healthy thing to have around. The more trash in the city streets, the more you're likely to see them crawling around looking for a snack.

HEY, MOVE OVER!

Here are the most crowded cities in the world, with the highest number of people jammed into each square mile.

MANILA, PHILIPPINES—106,226 people per square mile. Let's hope they don't all breathe out at the same time!

CAIRO, EGYPT—94,840 people per square mile. Wow, that's a lot!

LAGOS, NIGERIA—51,800 people per square mile. It gets very hot there. Imagine the smell of all those sweaty socks...

But... the world's smallest country, the **VATICAN CITY**, in Italy, has only 800 people in it.

There's a famous myth that escaped alligators live in the sewers under New York, but it's not true. Pity, because it's a great story!

Mom, I'm going to be late for school!

I need a pee!!!

stop, start... The city of Sao Paulo in Brazil has the world's **worst traffic jams**, sometimes stretching as far back as 120 miles.

WORST IN THE WORLD

These really rotten places have been turned into disgusting dirty dumps by pollution.

Stinky stack

Garbage smells bad because bacteria munch away on it, making lots of stinky gases as they eat (see page 84 for more about bacteria).

Trashy river

The shameful title of "**most polluted river in the world**" goes to the Citarum in Indonesia. It's choked by the trash and sewage of 9 million people who live in the area, plus more than 500 factories pumping out effluent (chemical-filled liquid). You can no longer see the water under a moving carpet of garbage. **Boatmen** still go on the river, but not to fish. Instead they risk catching diseases to sort through the garbage, looking for something they can sell.

What a dump... I love it!

Losing lake

Some lakes are so full of chemicals the water would burn your skin if you went swimming in it! One of the most polluted lakes in the world is Onondago Lake in New York State. Swimming and fishing are banned there because so much industrial waste floats in its waters, along with sewage. The local government is working hard to reverse the damage and make the lake safe.

Vile vacation zones

We wouldn't recommend a visit to these polluted places...

☢ Residents choke on the coal dust in the air of Linfen, China, said to be the most polluted city on the planet.

☢ In Ranipet, India, the water in local rivers has been made so toxic by factory waste that it stings like an insect bite if it touches human skin.

☢ In Sumgayit, Azerbaijan, more than 40 factories used to pump out chemicals, leaving behind tons of waste.

☢ The Pacific Ocean between Hawaii and Japan is home to the Great Pacific Garbage Patch, a vast soup of trash that's been washed into the ocean and then trapped together by whirling currents.

Some ocean areas are "dead zones," which means that nothing can live there because of an oxygen shortage caused by pollution.

TRASHY MIRROR

Help to stop the world becoming one big garbage dump by reusing your stuff to make this trashy mirror. You could write the word 'Garbage!' on the bottom of the cardboard frame for an extra laugh when someone looks at themselves in your creation.

- One mirror tile (from your local hardware store)
- Enough thick cardboard to mak a frame for the tile
- White craft glue
- A collection of mini junk to stick on around the mirror. Use anything that's clean and isn't too heavy to stick on. You can also add photos, cartoons, or words from magazines.
- Duct tape
- Scissors
- Ruler
- String to hang mirror with (optional)

Measure the tile. Cut out a cardboard frame that will give you plenty of room to stick your junk. Cut a hole in the cardboard frame slightly smaller than the mirror tile. You might need to use a craft knife and an adult to help you do this bit.

1

2

Glue the tile over the hole in the cardboard frame and leave it to dry. Then add duct tape around the edges for extra security.

Start arranging your junk on the card. When you are happy, glue all the pieces in place and leave it to dry.

3

4 If you want to hang your mirror, use duct tape to stick the string to the back of the mirror tile. Bend the ends of the string to make a triangle and use at least three pieces of duct tape to stick it on.

Rags to riches!

It's good to recycle as much as you can to keep the world clean. Here are some more ideas for making disgusting things from disgusting trash...

✱ Use your old clothes to make a freaky scarecrow. If you don't need to scare away birds from where you live, use it to scare away your friends at Halloween.

✱ Label a big empty box as your "rags to riches" store and ask your family to leave clean empty packaging in there. Glue these together to make models, such as giant bugs or scary aliens.

✱ Glue or tape clean trash together to make weird sculptures—perhaps a cardboard city called "waste world" or a mutant creature called "pollution monster."

House of Horrors

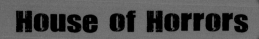

Bedtime Beasties

Anyone unlucky enough to get bedbugs in their home will be itching to get rid of them! The answer is to call in experts to zap them with chemicals. Here's the lowdown on those low-down, people biters.

Bedbug hunt

A good way to hunt for bedbugs is to look out for the blackish spots they leave around them when they poop.

Bedbug file

Here's some nighttime reading that'll make you squirm.

Description: Small wingless insect about ¼ inch long, brownish in color and flat, so it can crawl into tiny spaces.

Feeding habits: Sucks the blood of warm-blooded animals, such as humans and their pets.

Habitat: Found in cracks and crevices, especially in places where humans or pets sleep.

Important body parts: Skin-piercing mouthparts that inject fluid to help the bedbug suck up blood. This fluid makes a bedbug bite itch and swell.

Behavior: Bedbugs come out at night to feed.

Who stole the bedsheets?

The bedbug-lars!

WANTED!

Bedbug hideouts

Bedbugs live all around the world, except for cold, dry places, such as mountains. They like to live where people sleep a lot, so hotels are a good location for them. People who travel can unknowingly bring them back to their homes, and soon find their own bedrooms infested. It doesn't mean their homes are dirty, just that they've been unlucky. The bugs lurk on headboards and in mattress seams, but also around the edges of carpets and on drapes—any crevice that is dark and quiet.

Did you know that bedbugs hate pajama parties? They won't bite through pajamas, though they will look for a way to crawl inside...

Not so easy to get rid of us!

Let's go back to bed.

Bedbug secrets

These nighttime nasties have some shocking secrets:

❖ If bedbugs get vacuumed up, they'll soon **crawl out** of the **vacuum cleaner**, unless the vacuum bag is emptied into the garbage can outside.

❖ If your neighbor's house has bedbugs, they're quite likely to spread around the neighborhood, and that means you! Sweet dreams!

❖ Bedbugs prefer biting bare skin to hairy skin. People don't usually get bitten on the head (unless they're bald).

❖ Bedbugs shed their skin sometimes, leaving white flaky papery stuff lying around.

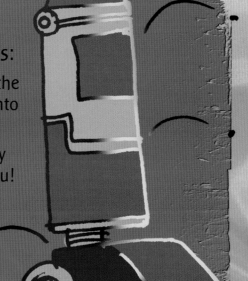

MIGHTY MITES

You drop skin flakes all the time (see page 80), which is good news for the millions of miniscule dust mites living in your house because they live off skin flakes. To them, you're a giant walking cookie, dropping tasty crumbs!

Feel proud

The amount of skin flakes you drop each day is enough to feed at least a million dust mites.

It's lucky we're so small, huh?

Sure is, you ugly mug!

Pass me a skin flake, would you?

Meet the mites

Dust mites are only 1/50 inch long. They look like tiny pincushions with eight legs. They live in dark places where they can get moisture and skin flakes to eat. Their favorite spot to hang out is in bed mattresses because there are lots of lovely skin flakes there, and moisture (sweat and drool) from sleeping humans. They don't bite and they don't do any harm

Why your vacuum smells

A full vacuum cleaner bag has a special smell all of its own. That's caused by the dust mites and mite poop you've hoovered up. When a mite munches on a skin flake, it secretes (releases) a chemical called an enzyme to help break down the flake and make it easier to eat. Some of the enzymes come out in the mite's tiny droppings (no bigger than pollen grains), which lie around the house or float in the air. The enzymes are what makes that vacuum smell.

Filthy facts

Who would have thought such tiny creatures would have such a big yuck factor…

❖ Dust mites live only for a couple of months, but during that time they make up to 200 times their own body weight in poop.

❖ Between 2 and 3 million mites live in the average bed mattress.

❖ Dust mites don't have stomachs.

❖ Dust mites are one of the main causes of asthma.

Dust mites don't like high temperatures, so make sure you wash bedding at 140°F or more to kill them off. **Sunlight** kills them, too.

HOME FOR DINNER!

Little critters could be eating away at your carpets, books, and clothes!

WELCOME

If you get mysterious holes in your clothes, it could be the larvae of clothes moths dining on your stuff in your drawers and closet!

Cuddly they ain't

Did you know that wooly bears could be brunching on your carpet? No, they're not cute teddy bears hiding behind your sofa. They're actually the larvae (babies) of an insect called a **carpet beetle**. They're brown and hairy, about ¼ inch long, and love chomping on wool. They get accidentally brought into houses on furniture or new carpet, or they might come from birds' nests in the roof.

Why was the moth so unpopular?

He picked holes in everything.

What did the furniture beetle say to the chair leg?

It's been nice to eat you!

A fish on your floor

Have you ever seen a weird, gray, little wormlike creature on your floor or in your bathtub, which darted away really fast when you got close? It's a kind of insect with no wings and three bristly tails, called a **silverfish**. It comes out at night and likes to eat anything starchy, such as paper, cereal, books, and wallpaper. You can tell if a silverfish has been munching on paper because it leaves a yellow-colored stain.

Soapy snacker

Silverfish will even eat bath soap, shaving foam, and shampoo.

Home sweet home
(with a side order of wood)

They say "Home Sweet Home"…Well, here's a list of minibeasts that would find parts of your house delicious!

Furniture beetle: Will tunnel through wood and paper. Won't harm you unless you are reading this book wearing a wooden leg…

Deathwatch beetle: Eats wood. If you hear a weird ticking noise at night, it could be this beetle trying to attract a mate (or it could be your alarm clock).

Powderpost beetle: Eats wood and then poops it out as little piles of dust.

Book louse: Feeds on musty old books. The glue in the spine is a special treat.

BATHROOM BUDDIES

Creatures may sometimes drop in to keep you company in the bathroom. Oh, and poisonous mold and living slime, too...

I'm ready for my bath now.

Soapy spiders

Have you ever looked into your bathtub and seen an eight-legged hairy monster looking right back at you? Did that insolent **spider** crawl up the **drain**? Don't panic. There aren't millions of spiders in your pipes. Spiders couldn't climb up the pipe beneath the plug because it has sections of water in it and they can't swim. Your creepy visitor will have dropped down into the bathtub, probably from the ceiling. Then, because the sides of the bathtub are shiny and slippery, it won't have been able to climb out.

Be nice to house spiders

Harmless house spiders are good for your home because they eat pest, such as flies.

Moldy poison

Sometimes **black mold** starts to grow on bathroom walls, slowly spreading and eventually beginning to smell. Mold is caused by tiny plantlike organisms called fungi. They love damp and will eat wallpaper, wall material, and wood. When some bathroom molds grow, they make chemicals called mycotoxins, designed to stop other types of mold from growing nearby. This is poisonous stuff and the smell of it can give humans headaches and dizziness.

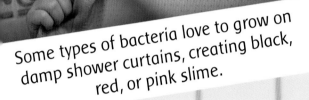

Some types of bacteria love to grow on damp shower curtains, creating black, red, or pink slime.

Bath-time bacteria

❖ The bathroom is such a warm wet place, it's like a tropical **vacation paradise for bacteria**. Millions of them share your bathroom, but don't worry. They won't peek!

❖ **Bathroom slime** made by bacteria is called "biofilm." It's not only found on shower curtains, but in showerheads and around faucets, too.

❖ The bacteria that makes bathroom slime loves to live in the pipes and filters of hot tubs, and can cause health problems if the hot tub isn't kept properly clean.

❖ A kind of bacteria that loves methane gas lives on shower curtains, too. It gets the yummy methane from munching on the curtain plastic.

❖ Bacteria get on **damp sponges** and facecloths and make them smell. When a sponge starts to stink like rotting garbage, it's time to chuck it out or put it in the washing machine.

HOUSE HUNTING

Being a minibeast isn't easy in your house. While you're relaxing, reading this book, vicious insect killers are on the loose nearby, out to get a juicy bug meal.

Pincher bugs

Earwigs will nip humans if they are scared. It hurts a bit but it's not dangerous.

'Ere's an earwig

Earwigs come out at night and eat other insects, insect eggs, and even each other. They like exploring, so you may find them in all sorts of unlikely places. They got their name because it was once thought they crawled into peoples' ears and burrowed into their brains. This is completely untrue, thank goodness. It's rare for an earwig to accidentally crawl into an ear, and if it did it wouldn't get far.

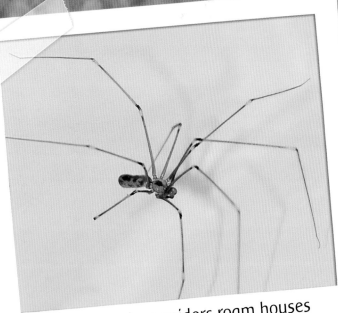

Daddy longlegs spiders roam houses hunting down insects, other spiders, and even other daddy longlegs!

I think I'll go hunting in the kitchen today.

Run away! Here comes the centipede!

The house centipede may be small, at about an inch long, but it's a vicious hunter of other creatures. It can run really fast on its **many pairs of legs**, even up walls and upside down on ceilings! It kills its prey by injecting venom with its fangs—it can nip humans, too, but not harmfully. Centipedes roam the house looking for spiders, bedbugs, ants, cockroaches, and silverfish.

Why was the centipede dropped from the football team?

He took too long to put his boots on.

Filthy facts

❖ The insect hunters in your house help keep the number of creepie-crawlies down, so maybe they're not so bad, after all.

❖ Daddy longlegs spiders don't have many enemies. Most of them die in the vacuum cleaner.

❖ The colossus earwig grows over 2 inches long.

❖ A daddy longlegs spider catches its prey by throwing some web at it. Then it weaves a web cocoon around the helpless victim, makes a hole in the web, and bites the doomed insect with its poison fangs.

❖ In Japan, house **centipedes** are kept as **pets**. They're called "gejigeji."

KITCHEN CRITTERS

If you don't keep your kitchen clean or store food properly, you could soon be sharing your kitchen with some other hungry horrors.

Runny 'roaches

You can sometimes spot where lots of cockroaches have been because they leave brown poop skid marks behind.

Crunchy cockroaches

If you ever walk barefoot into your kitchen one night and feel something crunching under your toes, you'll know you've got **cockroaches**! Dirty kitchens make the best cockroach spots because they like eating kitchen grease and food crumbs. The trouble is, roaches carry lots of germs and spread them around wherever they go. They also leave a lot of poop behind and they like cockroach company, which means that where there's one cockroach, there are usually many more nearby!

What's a cockroach's favorite movie?

Grease!

Filthy facts

❖ Cockroaches have been said to climb on men while they're asleep, and drink moisture off their mustaches!

❖ There are about 4,560 species of cockroach.

❖ Insect food pests include grain and flour beetles, biscuit beetles, flour moths, and even bacon beetles.

❖ If you can see lots of black dots in flour, the chances are you're looking at mites. Bon appétit!

❖ People in contact with flour mites may get a skin rash called "baker's itch."

It's a stowaway!

In past times, sailors on long journeys always tapped their biscuits before they ate them to get rid of biscuit beetle larvae living in them.

Mighty mites

There's a branch of the mite family that likes nothing better than to snack on food, preferably stale and damp. They're almost too tiny to see, but under a microscope they're pretty freaky creatures, with see-through bodies, wiggly legs, and hairy bristles. You might attract food mites if you keep flour, breakfast cereals, rice, dried fruit, or dried pet food for too many months or let it get damp. If flour is very heavily infested with food mites, it appears **to move on its own** in the package, as if it's alive!

FLOUR

How Disgusting Is Your House?

Arm yourself with a notebook and pen and get ready for some totally disgusting investigations to see how yucky your house is. Then reveal your shock results to the rest of the people in your house.

Smell science

Things smell if they give off stinky molecules that float into the air and get into your nose (find out more on page 41). Nose around and discover the smelliest things in your house.

Make a checklist :

* Smelliest food

* Smelliest shoes (and who they belong to)

* Smelliest room

* Smelliest garbage can or wastepaper basket

* Best-smelling room

* Best-smelling food

* Best overall smell you've ever had in the house

* Worst overall smell you've ever had in the house

CREEPY-CRAWLIE FILE

Investigate where the creepy-crawlies are likely to be hiding in your house.

* Dustiest place (where the most house dust mites are likely to be)

* Greasiest place (where grease-eating creepy-crawlers are likely to hang out)

* Place with the most cobwebs (look for spiderwebs in room corners or closets)

SCORE YOUR HOUSE

* Is your house modern or old?

Score 1 for "old," 0 for "new".

* Do you have a pet?

Score 1 for yes, 0 for no.

* Do you have an outdoor building (such as a shed or garage)?

Score 1 for yes, 0 for no.

* Do you have a closet under the stairs?

Score 1 for yes, 0 for no.

* Do you keep your room neat?

Score 1 for no, 0 for yes.

* Do you know where the duster is kept in your house? (Don't ask, just answer truthfully).

Score 1 for yes, 0 for no.

* Is your vacuum cleaner currently more than halfway full?

Score 1 for yes, 0 for no.

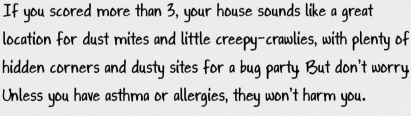

If you scored more than 3, your house sounds like a great location for dust mites and little creepy-crawlies, with plenty of hidden corners and dusty sites for a bug party. But don't worry. Unless you have asthma or allergies, they won't harm you. Try charging them rent!

HOUSEGUESTS FROM HELL

In some parts of the world, the oddest houseguests arrive—with fangs, claws, or poisonous bites!

Move over, Goldilocks

In Nevada, there was a spate of **burglar brown bears** breaking into houses to find food.

Toilet terrors

Imagine sitting on the toilet when it suddenly croaks, hisses, or squeaks! The **toilet makes a cozy place for some animals** to hide. Snakes are occasionally found curled up asleep in there, and in New South Wales, Australia, frogs decided to live in some of the local public restrooms. So many of them hopped into the toilets they stopped them from working. Rats are also regularly found in toilets, having swum up the pipes, or jumped in from above. They're really good underwater swimmers, so plumbing is no problem for them.

Anybody home?

Bad bears

A polar bear might knock on your door in Churchill, Canada. Polar bears hang out on the icy Arctic plain nearby, and sometimes wander into town looking for a meal. They raid trash cans or, if they smell something tasty cooking, they might even break into a house. There's a special bear rescue service that rounds them up without doing them harm and puts them in a **"polar bear jail,"** ready to go back out into the wild.

Look before you take a leak in an Australian outhouse, in case a deadly poisonous redback spider is nesting there.

Houseguests of horror

Here are some true-life horrible houseguests:

❖ In Florida, a lady found an 8-foot-long alligator in her kitchen chasing her cat.

❖ The Kenyan President's house was once **invaded** by **35 monkeys** who smelled the delicious cooking and wanted to share supper.

❖ Stray dogs became a problem when lots of them decided to live at Tanzania's airport, and hung around on the runways.

❖ Locals in Florida would prefer it if Cuban tree frogs got out of their bathrooms. They often climb up the toilet pipes and go swimming in the toilet bowl.

ROTTEN RODENTS

If rats and mice ever set up home in your house, you'd better get on the phone to the experts to get rid of them. That's if they haven't chewed through your phone lines!

Super rat!

Rats can get in just about anywhere they want. They can climb walls, fall great heights, squeeze through pipes, and swim through plumbing pipes. The females are champion breeders, giving birth every couple of months to lots of babies. And they'll eat just about anything, even electric cords. So it's best not to encourage wild rats by leaving big stores of food lying around.

Munching mice

Do you have tiny footprints in your butter dish and bites in your chocolate bar? Sorry to disappoint you, but you probably don't have fairies. It's more likely to be **mice**. You can tell they've arrived because they leave droppings and telltale signs of nibbling. They like high-fat foods, so mouse catchers often set their **traps** with tempting tastes, such as **bacon, peanut butter, and chocolate**. The greedy mice take their last luxury mouthful and get whacked by the trap.

Mice nest under the floor and in wall spaces, and can squeeze through cracks as small as ¼ inch to get into your house.

More where that came from

Rats usually only come out at **night**. If you see a rat in daytime, it's a sign there are lots of rats in the area—or it might just be hungry!

Poop patrol

If you see some suspicious droppings, here's how to tell which mini pooping monster you have lurking nearby. Don't touch the stuff. Get in the experts whose job it is to get rid of the critters doing the jobbies.

Mouse droppings: Black and about ¼ inch long, shaped like long, thin jelly beans.

Brown rat droppings: Like mouse poop but three times the size.

Black rat droppings: More sausage-shaped, fatter jelly beans.

Cockroach droppings: Tiny black specks.

Bat droppings: Like mouse droppings but shiny, speckled, and always found in a pile.

What you need
→

- Scrap cardboard, such as an empty cereal box
- Pencil or pen
- Scissors
- Cellophane tape and pencil or drinking straw
- Flashlight

MONSTERS IN THE DARK!

Next time your friends come over for a sleepover, get a scary surprise ready. Tell them you've noticed some unusually big, yucky-looking spiders or rats hanging around in your house. Then, just as they're going to sleep, spring a shadow surprise on them that'll make them scream!

FOR THE SCARY SPIDER

1 Draw a picture of a spider on the cardboard. Add holes for eyes, and some jagged teeth, then cut it out.

2 Tape a pencil or a drinking straw onto the back of the spider shape.

3 Put the lights out. Hold the spider up near the wall, and shine the flashlight on it to throw a big spider shadow on the wall. Wake up your friend for a look!

FOR THE ROTTEN RAT

1 Draw a rat shape with pointy teeth and paws with claws, and cut out two finger holes in it. Stick your fingers in the holes, hold it up to make a shadow, and make it scuttle along.

Something under the bed...

Did you ever think there was a monster under your bed? If it really was living down there, what kind of monster would it be? Here are some ideas:

✻ **Shoe nibblers**
If you leave smelly shoes under your bed, you could become infested with shoe nibblers, who love to snack on cheesy footwear.

✻ **Droolers**
Do you ever find drool on your pillow in the morning? Perhaps the drooler paid you a visit in the night and dripped on you while you were dreaming!

✻ **Duvet pullers**
If your covers fall off in the night, it's possible there might a duvet puller under the bed. Teach it a lesson by tugging the covers back again!

Don't worry. We made all these silly monsters up...or did we??!!

SOMETHING'S EATING YOUR HOUSE!

Don't panic, but something yucky could be eating into your house from the outside!

> We had an animal attack!

Face it, that's gross

A New York beauty parlor offers bird poop face masks. They say it lightens the skin.

Attack of the bird poo

Bird poop isn't just smelly and messy. It's full of acid that eats into brickwork and damages it. So if you get lots of birds nesting on the outside of your house, you'll also get piles of stone-destroying doo-doo. If the family car is parked nearby, the birds might well drop some poop on it, too, which damages the paintwork. Pigeons and seagulls are the worst offenders.

Am I boring you?

Something could be laying eggs in your house walls! In some countries, a type of bee called a **masonry bee** nests in gaps and holes it finds in brickwork. The bees keep on boring into the brickwork over the years, and eventually make so many tunnels in the stone that pieces start to fall off. Meanwhile birds come along to eat the bee babies hiding in the holes, and peck out some more stone. Eventually, you could get more holes than house!

In hot countries, termites may attack buildings and chomp up all the woodwork.

It wasn't me. It was the...

Do you sometimes get blamed for stuff that happens in your home? Next time your mom accuses you, tell her about these house monsters. If she says they don't exist, reply that they're too tiny to see, they come out at night, and you read about them in this book...So it *must* be true!

The untidy mite: Makes untidiness everywhere, particularly in children's bedrooms. It's always throwing clothes on the floor, looking for socks to eat.

The toothpaste-squeezing spider: Makes a mess with toothpaste by bouncing up and down on the tube. Come on! You could do some really big bouncing with eight legs.

The towel-dropping beetle: Makes a heap of wet towels on the floor of the bathroom, so it can suck the water out (and so it can have a laugh when humans get the blame for the mess).

The gross bug: Infests all houses where there are children, messing up any room it can by spilling and smearing. Signs of the gross bug include sticky doorknobs and unflushed toilets.

- Piece of thick cardboard about 8½ inches x 11 inches
- Pencil
- Scissors
- Paper towels
- White craft glue
- Paint and paintbrush
- Curly pasta shapes
- Hi-tack foam mounting tape

LIGHT SWITCH GARGOYLE

Gargoyles—ultra-ugly critters made of stone—were often carved on churches in medieval Europe to ward off evil spirits. What a great idea to have one in your room to scare off people you don't want visiting. They'll think twice when they come to switch your light on when you're not there!

1

Measure the light switch in your room and draw the shape in the middle of your cardboard, near the bottom. Leave enough room for the chin. Your light switch plate might be a different shape to the one in this book, but it doesn't matter. Make your gargoyle to fit your own.

2

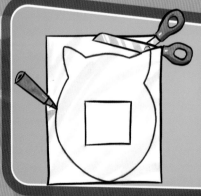

Design a gargoyle head round the light switch hole, which will be its mouth. Cut around the outline of the head. Draw on the eyes, nose, and mouth and some lines for the cheeks and chin.

3

Tear a piece of paper towel in half and twist it into a hotdog with pointed ends. Glue it over the lines you drew on. You will need to hold it in place for a minute until the glue starts to dry. Let it dry.

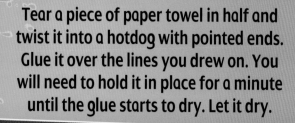

4 Tear up smaller pieces of kitchen paper. Dab white craft glue over the whole face and press the paper towel pieces over the top. Stick the curly pasta on top for the hair.

Once the gargoyle is completely dry, trim the edges to make them neat and paint over everything. A gray stone color with dark edging would make it look authentic. Let it dry, then secure it to the wall using the hi-tack foam mounting tape. **5**

Did you know that...
Gargoyles used to be designed so that they looked like they were having a pee when it rained. Seriously.

Freaky Food

Stomach Stuffing

Everybody needs food, but some people just don't know when to stop shoveling it in.

Sumo wrestlers eat two giant meals of meat stew each day to get heavy enough to fight.

Pop!

In very rare cases, the stomach can rupture from massive over-eating, flooding the body with deadly bacteria!

Hogs in history

Emperors were history's biggest hogs. Spanish Emperor Charles V ate a **whole chicken** for breakfast at 5 a.m., had a 20-course dinner at noon, then added two suppers at 5 p.m. and midnight. Apparently, he often complained of indigestion… Well, doh! The Roman Emperor Nero usually started eating dinner in the afternoon and finished around dawn. Eating so much at a **Roman feast** must have taken some doing, because dishes included yucky-sounding recipes, such as jellyfish, boiled tree fungi, and flamingo.

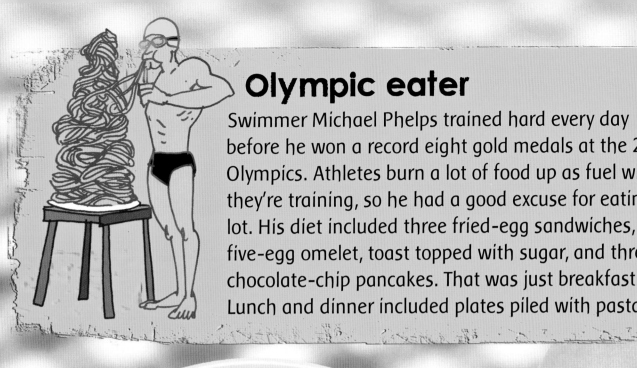

Olympic eater

Swimmer Michael Phelps trained hard every day before he won a record eight gold medals at the 2008 Olympics. Athletes burn a lot of food up as fuel when they're training, so he had a good excuse for eating a lot. His diet included three fried-egg sandwiches, a five-egg omelet, toast topped with sugar, and three chocolate-chip pancakes. That was just breakfast. Lunch and dinner included plates piled with pasta.

Burp-fest!

Eating contests are popular in the United States, with big-money prizes. Here are a few incredible eating records set during various contests. Don't try any of this at home.

Chicken nuggets: 80 in 5 minutes.

Hard-boiled egg eating: 65 in 6 minutes 40 seconds.

Cheese sandwiches: 26 in 10 minutes.

Burgers: 103 in 8 minutes.

Waffles: 29 in 10 minutes.

Cow brains: 57 in 15 minutes. (This weird record was set by Japanese champion Takeru Kobayashi, who also won a hotdog-eating contest when he ate 50.5 hotdogs in 12 minutes. While he wolfed them down, pieces of hotdog started coming out of his nose.)

Revenge of the Stomach!

If you stuff your stomach full of food too quickly, it's gonna bite back...

Exercising too quickly after you eat can give you indigestion, or even make you vomit, so it's best to rest for a little while after a meal.

George and the acid attack

We all get indigestion sometimes. Here's a story that explains why:

Once upon a time, a boy called George finished off some pepperoni pizza and fries in record time.

Soon his stomach began to hurt. He tasted horrible, sickly liquid in the back of his throat and he couldn't stop burping. George had eaten way too fast, and now he was paying the price...indigestion!

Because George ate too much too quickly, his stomach couldn't cope with the workload of breaking it all down (see page 66 for more). And what he ate was fatty and spicy, which a stomach has to work harder than usual to deal with.

The acid churning around in his stomach splashed up his esophagus (the tube between the mouth and the stomach) and he got a yucky taste of it, as well as getting pains in his belly.

George had to rest for a while until he felt better, and he had to say no to dessert!

194

Tummy nerves

Being nervous or anxious about something can give you indigestion.

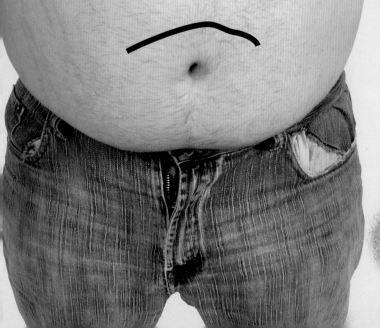

Bloaty burps

Food sometimes causes another yucky-sounding tummy complaint called **bloat**. When your stomach breaks down food it creates gas (see page 68). If there's a lot of gas, it gets trapped inside you for a while, until you burp or fart it out. A stomach full of gas begins to swell up, or "bloat," like a balloon. Carbonated drinks and beans are well-known gas-makers that can make you bloat.

Pardon!

Here are some bubbly facts about gas and wind:

❖ In some countries, it's polite to burp after a meal. People think it shows you enjoyed the food.

❖ Burps will usually smell of the food in your stomach.

❖ Sheep can have bloat if they eat the wrong type of grass. They can even die from it.

❖ Babies find it hard to get rid of gas and need help burping. Patting a baby on the back helps the burps to come out.

Stinking Scurvy

Here's why grown-ups never stop nagging about eating more fruit and vegetables...

Terrible taste

Sailors thought, wrongly, that they could ward off scurvy by eating mustard or drinking vinegar.

Vital vitamins

Food contains many different ingredients we need to stay healthy. A group of ingredients called vitamins is vital, and without them humans soon get sick. **Scurvy** is caused by lack of vitamin C, which we get from fresh fruit and vegetables. Until the 1800s, sailors didn't know what caused scurvy, and didn't take fresh fruit and vegetable supplies on voyages. Many got scurvy and had internal bleedings causing skin bruises and aches and pains, **teeth falling out**, **swollen gums**, madness, and even death. Remember that the next time you refuse to eat your fruit or vegetables!

If you eat me, you'll be sorry!

Sailors also sometimes got sick from eating polar bears' or seals' livers, both so full of vitamin A they are poisonous to humans.

Scurvy secrets

Sailors knew that if they went onshore and ate certain plants, such as a plant they called "scurvy grass," they'd keep scurvy at bay. They just didn't know why (the plants contained lots of vitamin C). They also thought they'd be cured by touching or smelling earth. Sometimes scurvy sufferers would go onshore, **dig a hole, and put their head in it**, which didn't work at all. Naval doctors finally worked out that the best way to stamp out scurvy was for ships to load up with lots of fresh citrus fruit (limes and lemons), a convenient way for the crew to get vitamin C every day.

SHUT UP AND EAT UP!

Sorry, but when adults keep blabbing about eating healthy foods, they're right. If you didn't, some disgusting things would happen to your body:

❖ If you ate no calcium, your bones would grow crookedly. Milk and fish contain lots of calcium.

❖ If you ate no iron, you would not have healthy blood. Iron is in meat, vegetables, and fruit.

❖ If you ate no protein, your muscles would waste away. Protein is in meat, eggs, cheese, and nuts.

❖ If you ate no vitamin A, you would get serious eye problems.

Eat your spinach, landlubbers!

GROSS GRUB IN HISTORY

Some truly horrible food has been eaten in the past.

Remove feathers before baking

It was once really common to eat seagull, either baked or in pies.

Besieged!

Over the centuries there have been many sieges, where an enemy sits outside a town or a castle waiting for the people inside to give up from starvation. The people inside had to eat whatever they could to survive. This has often included boiling and eating shoe leather, which contains protein (though it's very chewy). During the Siege of Leningrad in Russia in 1941–44, desperately hungry people even found a way to make flour from old wallpaper paste.

Chocolate for you?

The Aztecs invented chocolate, but their version was a bitter-tasting drink.

198

Awful Aztecs

The Mexican Aztecs had some disgusting dietary habits. They ate ants, grasshoppers, worms, and larvae, but their priests were the worst. They ritually sacrificed captured enemies, ripped their hearts out, and then ate parts of them. Archaeologists have found knife marks on bones, which prove that the Aztecs used to regularly do some people butchering. One of their favorite sacrifice recipes was a **human stew** called "tlacatlaolli."

Can't believe I ate those powdered pearls.

Filthy facts

❖ Medieval **plague cures** included eating powdered stag's horn, **powdered pearls**, and emeralds. None of these worked.

❖ In parts of North America, it was once common to eat **bear pie**.

❖ For centuries, people in Southeast Asia have eaten dog meat, believed to prevent disease.

TASTE IF YOU DARE

Your nose can fool you when it comes to smelly food. Try this taste experiment with your friend, and get them to do the test on you, too.

1 Place a blindfold over your friend's eyes, and ask them to shut their eyes, too.

2 Ask your friend to hold their nose each time you give them a piece of food. Keep a note of what you give them.

3 Ask your friend to guess what food they're eating. At the end, work out what they scored.

You'll be surprised at how many answers your friend got wrong. It's really hard to tell food apart with your nose and eyes shut because your body works out flavor not just by tasting but by smelling and feeling texture, too.

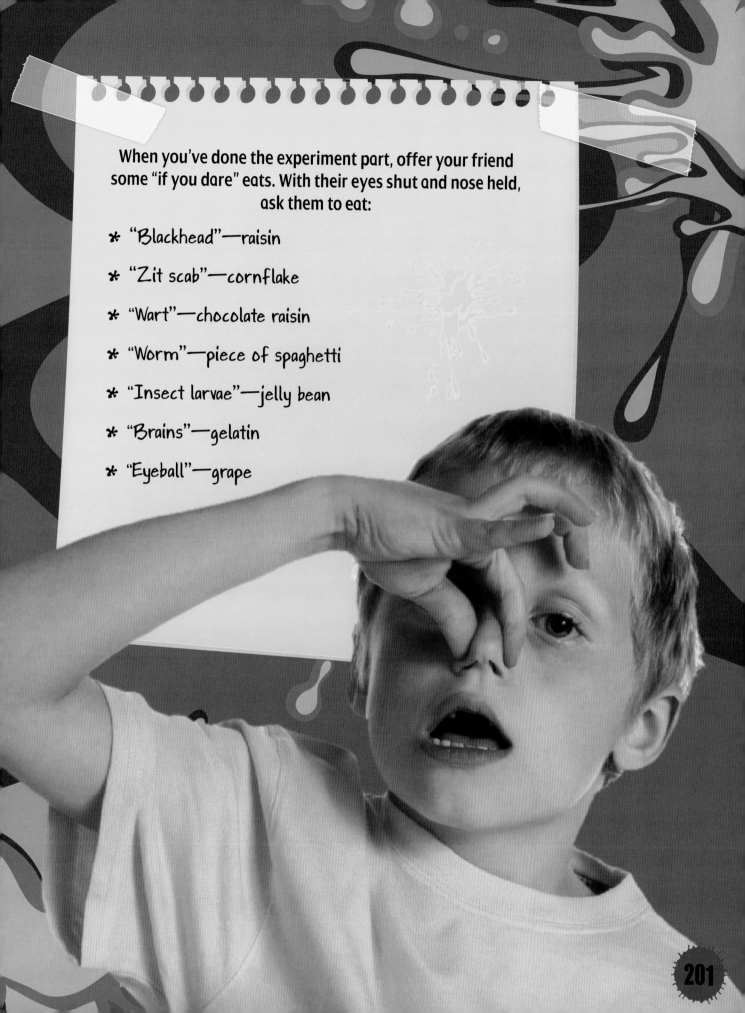

When you've done the experiment part, offer your friend some "if you dare" eats. With their eyes shut and nose held, ask them to eat:

* "Blackhead"—raisin

* "Zit scab"—cornflake

* "Wart"—chocolate raisin

* "Worm"—piece of spaghetti

* "Insect larvae"—jelly bean

* "Brains"—gelatin

* "Eyeball"—grape

WELCOME TO THE ROTTEN RESTAURANT

Some food is best eaten when it's rotten, perhaps with an extra sprinkling of maggots!

Sardinian **casu marzu** cheese has maggots put in it deliberately, and gets its special flavor from their poop.

Stinky shark

Rotten **shark** meat is an **Icelandic delicacy**. Here's how to make it. It sounds easy, except for step one…

1. Catch a shark.

2. Take out the shark's insides and cut up the meat that's left.

3. Dig a hole in some gravel and put the pieces in. Cover it with stones and leave for a couple of months. Dig the hole a good distance away from your house, because the meat starts to stink.

4. The juices will drain away from the shark, and it will start to rot. When it's soft and smells of really strong pee, take it out, wash it, and hang it up to dry.

5. Invite your friends around for a dinner to remember!

Don't try this at home

It's very dangerous to eat rotten meat (just in case you were thinking of trying), because it could make you very sick.

FILTHY FACTS

We've heard of rotten dinners, but this is going a bit far.

❖ You can tell when meat or fish start to rot because they begin to smell bad. The sick-making stink is caused by our old friends bacteria (see page 84).

❖ The Romans' favorite sauce was made from fish left so long it turned to mush.

❖ In the past, cider makers used to add some meat to their apple and water mixture. As the meat rotted, it helped the mixture turn into cider. They sometimes chucked rats into the cider vats.

❖ Casu marzu maggoty cheese (see opposite page) is officially banned in Italy because it can make people sick.

Gross game

Wild animal meat, such as deer and **wild birds** (such as pheasant), is called **game**. It's pretty tough and chewy, so it's hung up and left for a while to make it more tender. The longer it's left, the stronger it tastes, and some think it's best left until maggots (fly larvae) start to appear! The chef usually picks them off before cooking, but in Thailand you could be served **stinky meat**—game with the maggots still in it.

SMELLIEST FOOD

Get a whiff of these nose-tingling ingredients! If you put them all together for a picnic, the powerful odor would probably make you pass out.

Bombay duck is an Indian food famous for its silly name and its stink. It isn't a duck. It's a foul-smelling dried Indian fish.

Foul fruit

Yuk!

The world's smelliest fruit has to be the **durian**, a **spiky fruit** that grows in Southeast Asian countries, such as Thailand. It's said to smell like rotting garbage and it's banned from airplanes and train stations because of its sick stink. Under its hard skin, the flesh is soft and creamy, and it tastes nutty and sweet. The smellier the fruit, the better it's said to taste inside, and the more expensive it is to buy.

It's all in the name...

In Korea, "stinky tofu" is a popular snack, made of fermented soy beans, vegetables, and meat. It smells like a rotting garbage can.

Champion cheese stink

No, the **world's smelliest cheese** isn't that flaky stuff between your toes. It's the Vieux Boulogne cheese, made in northern France. We know this because a computer with an electronic nose smelled different cheeses and officially measured the smell of each one. The stinky champion is an orange color and after it's made it is kept in cellars for a few months before anyone eats it, just to ensure it's good and ripe.

Eeeeeurgh!

LOADS O' MONEY, LOADS O' SMELL

Some of the world's most expensive foods are also smelly or yucky sounding.

❖ The world's most expensive coffee, Kopi Luwak, is made from coffee beans eaten and then pooped out by an Asian wild cat called a palm civet. Cappuccino to go?

❖ White truffles are a type of edible fungi that grow under oak trees. They sell for thousands of dollars a pound. Some people think they smell fantastic. Others insist that they stink horribly. It'll cost you a lot of money to find out which side you're on!

❖ One of the world's most expensive foods is caviar—tiny, salted fish eggs. They're little, black grainy pieces, a bit like sections of blackberry (only fishy).

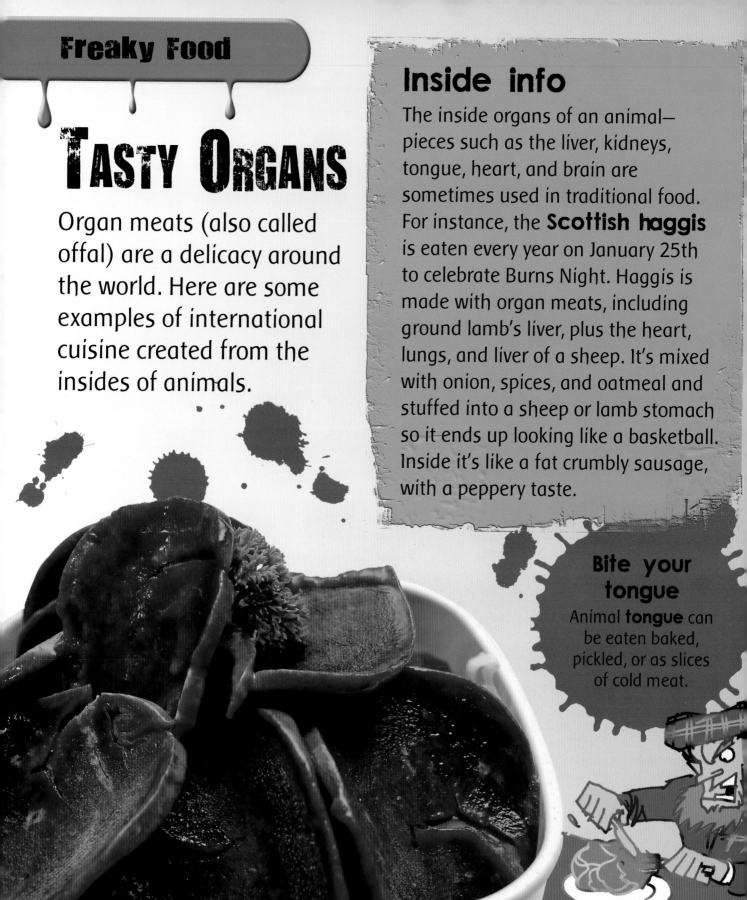

Tasty Organs

Organ meats (also called offal) are a delicacy around the world. Here are some examples of international cuisine created from the insides of animals.

Inside info

The inside organs of an animal—pieces such as the liver, kidneys, tongue, heart, and brain are sometimes used in traditional food. For instance, the **Scottish haggis** is eaten every year on January 25th to celebrate Burns Night. Haggis is made with organ meats, including ground lamb's liver, plus the heart, lungs, and liver of a sheep. It's mixed with onion, spices, and oatmeal and stuffed into a sheep or lamb stomach so it ends up looking like a basketball. Inside it's like a fat crumbly sausage, with a peppery taste.

Bite your tongue

Animal **tongue** can be eaten baked, pickled, or as slices of cold meat.

Tell me about tripe

Tripe is the rubbery lining of a cow's stomach, and it can be eaten when it's been cooked for a few hours. It looks like a piece of white tire rubber, and some say it tastes like that, too. You can buy it pickled or in cans, or fresh at the butcher's. There are different kinds, depending on which part of the stomach it comes from. There's blanket tripe from the first stomach, honeycomb tripe from the second stomach, or book tripe from the third.

Black pudding, a dish cooked all around Europe, is made from oatmeal, onions, and pig's blood stuffed into a pig's stomach lining.

On the organ meat menu tonight...

Here are some examples of international cuisine created from the insides of animals:

Brazil—Feijoada, a tray of meat including the ears, feet, and tail of a pig.

Singapore—Pig's organ soup.

Pakistan—Curried goat brain.

Lebanon—United States sandwich.

USA, Europe, and Australia—Head cheese (also called brawn). Meat from the head of a pig set in gelatin.

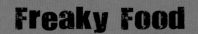

SUCK ON A SCORPION

Would you like a caterpillar kebab or a termite burger? There are more than a thousand edible creepy-crawlies.

How to cook moths

Each year thousands of bogong moths return to the Australian Bogong Mountains to breed. They used to be a delicacy for Aboriginal Australians, who would gather them and cook them. Here's how to cook a bogong moth:

❖ Cook them in salt and stir them around in hot ashes to get rid of their wings and legs.

❖ Sift them in a net to get rid of the heads.

❖ Grind them up into paste.

❖ Bake a cake and have a party!

Jiminy, that sounds good!

Some types of cricket are edible, though you have to remove the guts first.

Grubs are good eatin'

Lots of insects are packed with protein, especially fat baby larvae. Aboriginal Australians like to tuck into a witchetty grub, a big white moth larva the size of a finger. Meanwhile, in **Japanese restaurants**, you might be offered **boiled wasp larvae** or perhaps fried silk moth pupae. Some caterpillars are edible, too, and are good for you because they're high in iron. In Nigeria, powdered caterpillar gets sprinkled into soup.

Don't go eating creepy-crawlies yourself at home, because most are poisonous and will make you sick.

INSECT-EATING SECRETS

❖ Insects taste best when they are cooked or frozen alive.

❖ Insects with hard outer shells need to be boiled before eating.

❖ People in Bali, Indonesia, eat grilled dragonflies. They catch them with a stick coated in sticky plant juice.

❖ Locusts are best eaten cooked in saltwater and then dried out.

What you need →

Slug and Worm Cakes

Has all this talk of bug-eating made you hungry? Make some yummy cupcakes decorated with juicy, little garden critters. If you know a gardener who complains about slugs eating their plants, help them to get their revenge by giving them one of your sugar slugs to eat themselves!

(This recipe makes 12 cupcakes, buy store-bought cakes to decora

- Muffin pan
- Paper cake liners
- ½ cup butter
- ½ cup brown sugar
- ¾ cup self-rising flour, sifted
- 2 eggs
- 1 teaspoon vanilla extract
- Electric mixer or bowl and wooden spoon
- Teaspoon
- A friendly adult to help you with the hot parts of this recipe—putting the cakes in the oven and taking them out.

To make your cakes

1 Heat oven to 350°F. Beat the butter and sugar together until creamy.

2 Add the flour and eggs gradually, beating them in. Add the vanilla extract.

3 Spoon the mixture into 12 cupcake liners and bake for 15–20 minutes until golden. Let it cool.

What you need for grass, slugs and worms

◦ A pack of store-bought frosting
◦ A package of marzipan
◦ Green, red, and orange food coloring
◦ Teaspoon
◦ Knife
◦ Clean paintbrush

1 Break off a piece of frosting and mix it in a bowl with some green food coloring, to make grass.*

*It's hard to make a big amount at once, so do small portions at a time and decorate your cakes bit by bit.

2 Spread the "grass" on a cake and us a knife to pull bits up, making it look rough and grassy.

3 Break off a small slug-size piece of marzipan and press it into a slug shape that will fit on a cake. Pinch the marzipan to make a couple of tentacles. Use the knife to make ridges on the body. Paint the slug using the food coloring. (If you want, you can mix red and green to make brown.)

4 To make a wiggly worm, roll some marzipan between your clean hands. Dab some food coloring on with a toothpick to make eyes.

You could add pieces of marzipan on toothpicks for extra-big slug tentacles. If you like, brush the slug with jam or marmalade to make it look slimy

PEOPLE PIE, ANYONE?

In past times (and not so long ago), people sometimes had humans for dinner.

Powdered Egyptian mummy was once a popular medicine in Europe and North Africa, along with mummy molasses.

A sick story

There are several famous people-eating legends. Tantalus, son of ancient Greek god Zeus, takes the cake, though. Legend has it he **cut up** his son **Pelops**, **boiled him**, and **served him** to the gods for dinner. They refused to eat, except for a goddess called Demeter, who mistakenly ate Pelops' shoulder. A goddess called Fate saved Pelops by boiling up his pieces in a sacred pot. He came out mainly fine, but had to wear a false shoulder made of ivory for the rest of his life.

I think it's Uncle Peter for dessert.

212

Family feast

Cannibal communities were mainly found on isolated islands or in jungle areas. They have been found all over the world, in parts of the Pacific, Africa, and South America. After a battle, some cannibals ate the dead bodies of their enemies to supposedly kill off their spirit. Others ate the bodies of their dead relatives because they believed they would gain strength and wisdom from them.

Fatties preferred

In the African Congo, cannibals kept their captured enemies in cages to fatten them up before eating.

FILTHY FACTS

❖ The Korowai tribe in southeastern Papua were cannibals right up until the 1970s, when they met outsiders for the first time.

❖ In 12th-century Arabia, "mellified man" medicine is said to have been used. It was made from soaking a dead body in honey.

❖ Hot human blood, distilled brains, and powdered human heart have all been eaten as possible cures for epilepsy. None of them work.

❖ If you ever see "long pig" on a menu, run. It's a cannibal name for cooked human.

° Two packets of lime gelatin
° A clean, new dishwashing glove
° Pitcher
° Two binder clips
° Bucket
° Two sturdy sticks (dowels will do)
° Sharp scissors
° Red food coloring and brush
° Room in your freezer compartment

EDIBLE HAND

Make this yummy, rotten-looking hand and dare everyone to dig in. They'll find it's tastier than chewing nails. The project takes a couple of days, so make it early enough for a special occasion.

1 Wash the glove thoroughly. Set up the glove by clipping either side of it securely to the two sticks balanced on top of a bucket.

2 Make up the gelatin in the jug, as shown on the package, but with half as much water as you would normally use.

3 Carefully pour the gelatin into the glove. Let it set overnight.

4 Carefully unclip the glove and put it in the freezer. It will take about 36 hours.

5 Just before you want to serve your hand, take it out of the freezer and carefully cut off the glove. Don't worry if fingers break off. It'll look even more yucky!

6 Quicky dab on red fingernails and make the wrist stump red and any finger stumps red.

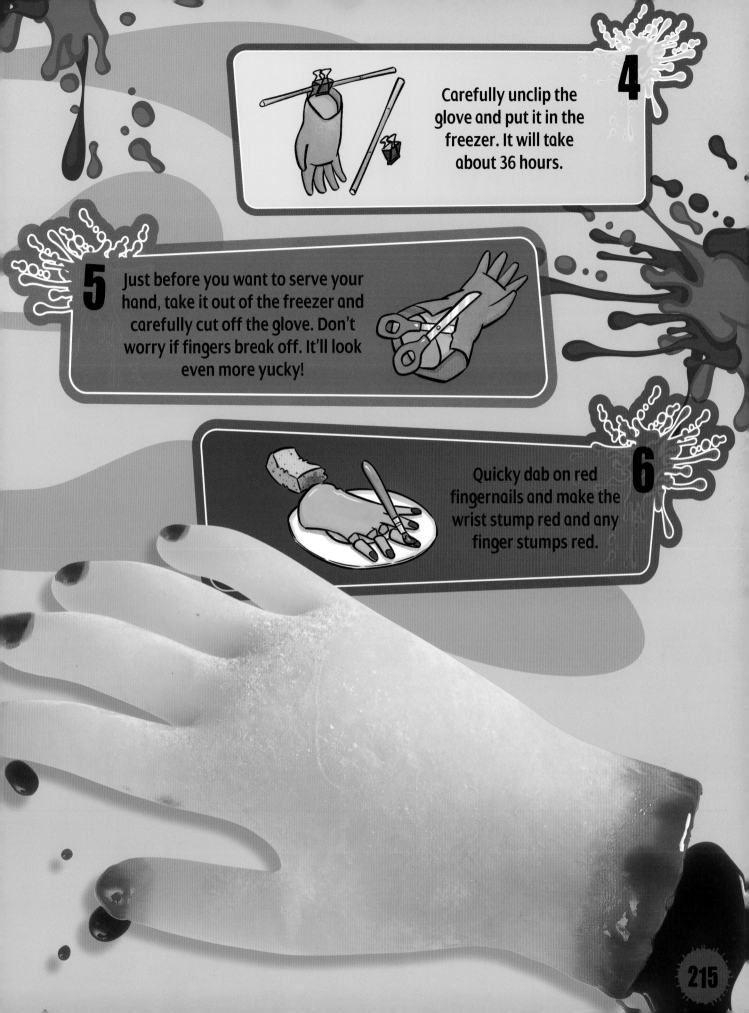

TERRIBLE TOP FIVES!

We've looked back over all the yucky facts in this book and come up with some terrible top five lists. See if you agree, and if you don't, make your own horrible selections!

History Smells

Top five messy jobs in history

We're guessing somebody had to do these awful tasks and have suggested some useful tips they might have needed to help them get through their disgusting day.

1. Chef for early cavemen
Top tip for this job: You will only have meat and bones to work with, so here are some recipe ideas: meat and bone burger, meat and bone soup, meat and bone platter, and bone surprise (the surprise is that you've run out of meat).

2. Cleaner at the Roman Colosseum, where gladiators hack one another to pieces
Top tip for this job: Don't look too closely into your dustpan and brush.

3. In charge of scraping out the brain at a mummy-making session in ancient Egypt
Top tip for this job: Remember to wash your hands before you eat your lunch.

4. Blackbeard the Pirate's hairdresser
Top tip for this job: Blackbeard likes to wear burning fuses in his hair when he goes into battle, so forget the hairspray and bring gunpowder and matches.

5. Henry the VIII's bum-wiper (his "groom of the stool")
Top tip for this job: Wear a smile on your face, a clothespin on your nose, and invent toilet paper quickly.

Sickening Science

Mission Control... Do we have any handy wipes?

Top five stinky gases

1. Hydrogen sulfide—Phew!
Rotten-egg smell found in farts.

2. Ammonia—Phwoar!
The smell of pee-covered toilets.

3. Methane—Puh-leez!
The smell of cow farts and garbage piles.

4. Methanethiol—Who did that?
Found in farts and on smelly feet.

5. Dimethyl sulfide—Yuck!
The smell of boiling cabbage.

Top five space station nightmares

1. Shower of space snot
An astronaut sneezes so hard his nose showers out floating boogers.

2. Cheesy floater alert
An astronaut spills a carton of sour milk and the blobs drift off around the station.

3. Space station snowstorm
An astronaut with dandruff shakes his head.

4. Air full of underwear
An astronaut drops a pile of dirty laundry.

5. Barf cloud
An astronaut suddenly gets a bout of space vomit.

Yucky You

All the facts in this book are carefully researched—all but these five complete lies about the human body, answering five of the top body questions that kids have. Wouldn't it be fun if they were true?

1. Why do people sneeze?

"To keep their nostrils from growing over."

2. Why is poop brown-colored?

"Because of all the chocolate we eat."

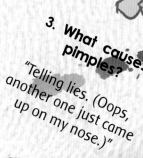

3. What causes pimples?

"Telling lies. (Oops, another one just came up on my nose.)"

4. What is spit made of?

"Brain juice."

5. Why does my stomach grumble?

"Your stomach monsters are hungry."

Terrible Top Fives

Animals... Aaaargh!

Top five smelly animals

1. Skunk
Sprayer of sickening stink juice.

2. Zorilla
An African skunklike animal and another sprayer of terrible smells.

3. Stink bug
Stinky by name, stinky by nature. Makes a smelly body liquid that keeps enemies away.

4. Cow
Cows are world-champion farters.

5. Human
Stinky feet, sweaty armpits, yucky burps—we have to be in the list!

Creepie-Crawlies Rule

Top five ways we wish we could copy creepie-crawlies

You've heard of Spiderman, right? He can shoot out web threads like a spider, and he got us thinking about five creepie-crawlie skills it'd be really useful for humans to have:

1. If you could jump up to 80 times your own body length, like a jumping spider...
... You could save on fuel by bouncing everywhere instead of going by car.

2. If you could taste food with your feet like a fly...
... You could try food and talk at the same time.

3. If you could make honey like a bee...
... You'd be even sweeter than you are now.

4. If you could carry your home around on your back like a snail...
... You could go camping without having to put up a tent.

5. If you could eat books like a book louse...
... You could snack on this book once you've finished with it.

Our Wonderful World

Top five smelliest places in the world

Here are five of the smelliest places in the world:

1. A jungle in Sumatra
Where the world's smelliest flower, the titan arum, grows. It smells like rotting flesh.

House of Horrors

Top five animal housepests

Here are five of the worst house critters around, and the reasons why they made our top five grade:

1. Bedbugs
Freaky little sickos that feed on people while they sleep.

2. Pet fleas
Because they can hop from pets onto humans and leave you scratching. Luckily for you, this book is heavy enough to double up as a flea squasher.

3. Earwigs
Because they have a scary name and horrible-looking pincer parts.

4. Furniture beetles
Because they would eat all your wood, if they could.

5. Spiders
Who invited them, anyway? They just show up and leave their webs lying around all over the place.

2. A cheese cellar in northern France
The cellars where Vieux Boulogne, the world's smelliest cheese, is stored.

3. Near a durian tree in Thailand
Where the world's smelliest fruit, the durian, grows. It is said to smell like a mixture of pig poop, onions, sweaty socks, and paintbrush-cleaner.

4. In a North American woodland
Anywhere near the home of a bad-tempered skunk.

5. In an athletics changing room at the Olympic Games
When the athletes take off their sweaty running shoes on a hot day, get outta there!

Freaky Food

Top five yucky foods

If you see these on the menu, say thanks, but you've eaten.

1. Casu marzu
A maggot-covered cheese that will leave your plate, and your flesh, crawling.

2. Tlacatlaolli
An Aztec stew made of human flesh. How hungry would you have to be to say "yes" to that?

3. Kopi luwak
A seriously sick cat-poop drink. Coffee made from beans pooped out by a civet cat.

4. Bogong
Mmmm, roasted moth! This is a type of moth that has turned up on the Aboriginal Australian menu.

5. Hakarl
Get your jaws around Jaws. This is fermented (rotten) shark, which is dried and then eaten in Iceland.

Index

Index

Acknowledgments

t = top, b = bottom, l = left, r = right, m = middle

Cover Boy: Ole Graf/zefa/Corbis, toad: Bob Elsdale/Getty, Tarantula: Martin Harvey/Getty, Cockroaches: GK Hart & Vikki Hart/Getty

1 Alex Gorodnitchev/Dreamstime.com, 6 (cockroaches) istockphoto, 6tl Kati Neudert/Dreamstime.com,6tr Pdtnc/Dreamstime.com, 6br Tommounsey/Dreamstime.com 7 Marilyn Nieves/istockphoto 8–9 David Hughes/Dreamstime.com, 10m Stefan Ataman/Dreamstime.com, 10b Paul Souders/Corbis, 11 Christophe Boisvieux/Corbis, 12–13 LemonCrumpet/Sharealike, 13 Kristian Sekulic/Dreamstime.com, 14–15 Liz McAulay/Getty, 16–17 David Monniaux/GNU, 16t Rachelle Burnside/Dreamstime.com, 20–21 Patti Gray/Dreamstime.com, 21t Dave Dunford, 22–23 Rcpphoto/Dreamstime.com, 23 Anthony Aneese Totah Jr/Dreamstime.com, 26 Rigaud, 27 Elena Elisseeva/Dreamstime.com, 28 LonghH/istockphoto, 29l Szefei/Dreamstime.com, 29r Ratstuben/istockphoto, 31 Bettmann/CORBIS, 32–33 Agg/Dreamstime.com, 33l Tommounsey/istockphoto, 33r Borg Mesch, 34–35 Michael Blann/Getty, 36 Vxovka/Dreamstime.com, 37 Jose Manuel Gelpi Diaz/Dreamstime.com, 38 Carolyn Seelen/Dreamstime.com, 39t Alina Isakovich/Dreamstime.com, 39b millerpd/istockphoto, 40 Steve Luker/Dreamstime.com, 41 Massimiliano Leban/Dreamstime.com, 44 Fdbphotography/Dreamstime.com, 45l Dreamstime.com, 45r Kirsty Pargeter/Dreamstime.com, 46–47 NASA 47t NASA, 50 Bertrand Collet/Dreamstime.com, 51l wsfurlan/istockphoto, 51r Greencrick/Dreamstime.com, 52 Batemcr/Dreamstime.com, 53t Li Shaowen/ChinaFotoPress/Getty Images, 53b Gene Blevins/LA Daily News/Corbis, 56–57 AFP/Getty Images, 57 WireImage/Getty, 58 NASA, 59t NASA, 59b NASA, 60–61 PM Images/Getty, 62 Stephen Coburn/Dreamstime.com, 63l Kati Neudert/Dreamstime.com, 63r Hixson/Dreamstime.com, 66l Jose Manuel Gelpi Diaz/Dreamstime.com, 66r princessdlaf/istockphoto, 66–67 Varyaphoto1000/Dreamstime.com, 67 Marilyn Nieves/istockphoto, 68 Photowitch/Dreamstime.com, 69t Najin/Dreamstime.com, 69b Stephane Duchateau/Dreamstime.com, 70l Kandasamy M/Dreamstime.com, 70tr Drx/Dreamstime.com, 70mr Beth van Trees/Dreamstime.com, 71t Robeo/Dreamstime.com, 71b Rohit Seth/Dreamstime.com, 72–73 Monika Wisniewska/Dreamstime.com, 73t Marilyn Barbone/Dreamstime.com, 73b Simone Van Den Berg/Dreamstime.com, 76 Braendan Yong/Dreamstime.com, 76–77 Kentannenbaum/Dreamstime.com, 77t Igor Dutina/Dreamstime.com 77b Simone Van Den Berg/Dreamstime.com, 80 emre ogan/istockphoto, 81 Ron Chapple Studios/Dreamstime.com, 82 Gregory F Maxwell/GNU, 83l Marzanna Syncerz/Dreamstime.com, 83r Sharon Dominick/istockphoto, 84–85 Ivan Cholakov/Dreamstime.com, 84b Monika Wisniewska/Dreamstime.com, 86t Renáta Krivanová/Dreamstime.com, 85m Jorge Salcedo/Dreamstime.com, 86–87 DLILLC/Corbis, 88t Karora, 88b Roger Whiteaway/ Dreamstime.com, 89 Andrei Calangiu/Dreamstime.com, 90–91 Carolina k. Smith/Dreamstime.com, 90lt Christopher Kennedy/GNU, 90b Ales Veluscek/istockphoto, 91t Adam Jastrzrbowski/Dreamstime.com, 91b Anke Van Wyk/Dreamstime.com, 94 Mairead Neal/Dreamstime.com, 95 Frank Greenaway/Getty, 96l Anthony Hathaway/Dreamstime.com, 96r Alex Gorodnitchev/Dreamstime.com, 97 Photomyeye/Dreamstime.com, 100 Eric Isselée/Dreamstime.com, 101l Alex Bramwell/Dreamstime.com, 101r Joe McDonald/CORBIS, 102 Miflippo/Dreamstime.com, 103t Mila Zinkova/GNU, 103b Aleksandr Bondarchiuk/Dreamstime.com, 106 David De Lossy/ Getty, 104–105 Blair Bunting/istockphoto, 107 Seriousguy/Dreamstime.com, 108–109 David Burder/Getty, 109 Shawn And Sue Roberts/Dreamstime.com, 110 Richard Griffin/Dreamstime.com, 111 Miroslava Kopecka/Dreamstime.com, 112–113 Wolfgang Kaehler/CORBIS, 114l Marc Dietrich/Dreamstime.com, 114r DaddyBit/istockphoto, 115t Göran Wassvik/Dreamstime.com, 115b Marek Kosmal/Dreamstime.com, 117t Paul Fleet/Dreamstime.com, 117b Bartek Sadowski/Dreamstime.com, 120–121 Phil Morley/Dreamstime.com, 121t Flagstaff fotos/GNU, 121b Chartchai Meesangnin/Dreamstime.com, 122 Janpietruszka/Dreamstime.com, 123t Pdtnc/Dreamstime.com, 123b Thesupe87/Dreamstime.com, 124–125 Zoran Ivanovic/istockphoto, 124 Bobby Deal/Dreamstime.com, 128l Michael & Patricia Fogden/CORBIS, 128b Clinton & Charles Robertson/GNU, 129 Kevin Dyer/istockphoto, 130 Christopher Badzioch/istockphoto, 131t Adam Gryko/Dreamstime.com, 132b Dreamstime.com, 132–133 Alexandru Magurean/istockphoto, 133l Alvesgaspar/GNU, 133r Rafa Irusta/Dreamstime.com, 134 Dmitrijs Mihejevs/Dreamstime.com, 135l Wolfgang Kure, 135r Richard Goerg/istockphoto. 138–139 Ariel Molina/epa/Corbis, 140–141 Kenneth McIntosh/istockphoto, 140t Michael Lynch/Dreamstime.com, 141 Martin Krause/Dreamstime.com, 144–145 Hashim Pudiyapura/Dreamstime.com, 144 Sergey Bondarenko/Dreamstime.com, 145 Laurent Hamels/Dreamstime.com, 148–149 Ryan Morgan/istockphoto, 148ml Bob Thomas/Popperfoto/Getty Images, 148bl Marc Dietrich/istockphoto, 148r saluha/istockphoto, 150–151 Jose Fuente/Dreamstime.com, 150l LOUOATES/istockphoto, 151 Paige Foster/Dreamstime.com, 152 Eric Nguyen/Corbis, 153b Demydenko Myhailo/Dreamstime.com, 154–155 Ander Gillenea/Getty Images, 155 Rui Gomes/Dreamstime.com, 156l Alexander Maksimenko/istockphoto 156r Martin Purmensky/Dreamstime.com, 157t Jay Prescott/Dreamstime.com, 157b Niko Fagerström/Dreamstime.com, 158–159b Stoupa/Dreamstime.com, 158 istockphoto, 159t istockphoto, 159b AFP/Getty Images, 160–161 Dennis M.Sabangan/epa/Corbis, 161l Stanislav Komogorov/Dreamstime.com, Petra Roeder/Dreamstime.com, 161r Rob Bouwman/istockphoto, 164–165 Kris Hanke/istockphoto, 166 US Federal Government, 167 Monika Adamczyk/Dreamstime.com, 168–169 Sebastian Kaulitzki/Dreamstime.com, 169 Janehb/Dreamstime.com, 170–171 Brad Calkins/Dreamstime.com, 170 Dawid Zagorski/Dreamstime.com, 171 Holger Leyrer/Dreamstime.com, 172 Eric Isselée/Dreamstime.com, 173t Jim Jurica/istockphoto, 173b Ryan Jones/istockphoto, 174t Alvesgaspar/GNU, 174b Fir0002/Flagstaffotos/GNU, 176 arlindo71/istockphoto, 177 Daniel Hughes/Dreamstime.com, 178–179 Ann Marie Kurtz/istockphoto, Mike Sonnenberg/istockphoto, 180–181 graham klotz/istockphoto, 180 Timur Arbaev/Dreamstime.com, 181l Renate Micallef/Dreamstime.com, 181r Stocksnapper/Dreamstime.com, 182–183 Dave White/istockphoto 182 Oleg Kozlov/Dreamstime.com, 183 Stefan Klein/istockphoto, 186–187 Krezofen/Dreamstime.com, 187 Michael Pettigrew/Dreamstime.com, 190–191 Lara Jo Regan/Getty, 192t Michael S. Yamashita/CORBIS, 192b Floortje/istockphoto, 193l Ruslan Nassyrov/Dreamstime.com, 193r Kati Neudert/Dreamstime.com, 194 Kathy Wynn/Dreamstime.com, 195 Ron Sumners/Dreamstime.com, 196–197 Michal Rozanski/istockphoto, 196 Tom Dowd/Dreamstime.com, 197 Giorgio Fochesato/istockphoto, 198–199 istockphoto, 198t Dschwen/GNU, 198b Niilo Tippler/istockphoto. 199l Ruslan Nassyrov/Dreamstime.com, 199r The Gallery Collection/Corbis, 202–203 Abel Leão/istockphoto, 202t Carol Spears/GNU, 202b Ruslan Nassyrov/Dreamstime.com, 203 Andrew Howe/istockphoto, 204t Aliced/Dreamstime.com, 204m Adam Gryko/Dreamstime.com, 204b Shariffc/Dreamstime.com, 206 Evan Wong/dreamstime.com, 207t Patrick SwanDreamstime.com, 207b istockphoto, 208t Donald Hobern/GNU, 208m Scowill/Dreamstime.com, 208b Nico Smit/Dreamstime.com, 209l Adam Gryko/Dreamstime.com, 212–213 Pavel Losevsky/Dreamstime.com, 212t Scott Rothstein/Dreamstime.com, 217 NASA, 219 istockphoto